The Gun

Cecil Scott Forester was born in Cairo in 1899 and educated at Alleyne's School and Dulwich College, afterwards studying medicine at Guy's Hospital. His first book, a crime novel entitled *Payment Deferred* (1926), was very successful and was dramatized. With his first wife he went inland voyaging in a dinghy through England, France and Germany, the log being published as *The Voyage of the 'Annie Marble'*, followed by *The 'Annie Marble' in Germany* (1936). In 1936–7 he was war correspondent for *The Times* in Spain. Others of his novels include *Brown on Resolution* (1929), *The Gun* (1933), and *The Ship* (1943). In *The Happy Return* (1937) he introduced one of the most popular heroes of modern fiction, Captain Hornblower, who appeared also in *Flying Colours* (1938), and *A Ship of the Line* (1939), which was awarded the Tait Black Memorial Prize. Later stories in the same series are *The Commodore* (1944), *Lord Hornblower* (1946), *Mr Midshipman Hornblower* (1950), and *Hornblower and the 'Atropos'* (1953). *Long Before Forty* (1967) is autobiographical.

C. S. Forester died in 1966.

Also by C. S. Forester in Pan Books

Payment Deferred
Lieutenant Hornblower
Hornblower in the West Indies
Brown on Resolution
Death to the French
Hornblower and the 'Atropos'
Hornblower and the Crisis
Plain Murder
The Man in the Yellow Raft
Gold from Crete

C.S.Forester

The Gun

PAN BOOKS LTD
In association with The Bodley Head

First published 1933 by The Bodley Head Ltd.
This edition published 1987 by Pan Books Ltd,
Cavaye Place, London SW10 9PG
in association with The Bodley Head
19 18 17 16 15 14 13 12 11
Printed and bound in Great Britain by
Hazell Watson & Viney Limited,
Member of the BPCC Group,
Aylesbury, Bucks

CHAPTER I

A DEFEATED army was falling back through the mountains from Espinosa. Such was its condition that an ignorant observer would find it easier to guess that it had been defeated than that it had been an army. The twenty thousand men of whom it was composed were strung out along twenty miles of road; its sick and its dead littered the edges of the road for a hundred miles to the rear. At the head came such of the cavalry as were fortunate enough still to have horses to ride; they felt safer there than in their proper place covering the retreat. Next came the infantry in groups, in herds, or in ones and twos. Their white Bourbon uniforms were now in strips and tatters, and the skin, blue with disease and cold, showed through the rents. Perhaps half of them still retained their muskets, and of these perhaps a quarter had bayonets as well. Here and there little groups still displayed some soldierly bearing, and marched steadily beneath the cased regimental colours, but these groups were few, for most of the colours had been lost at Espinosa.

The long column of misery tended continually to grow longer, as the more robust struggled forward to get as far as possible from the pursuing French, and as the weaker fell farther and farther behind. There were enough weaklings in all conscience; even in summer the men had been badly clothed, and even in victory insufficiently fed, and now it was winter, and Espinosa had been fought and lost, and the route of the retreat lay away from the fertile plains and up into the inhospitable mountains. The rain had fallen upon them in deluges for days, and now as they climbed higher it was turning into sleet, and a bitter cold wind blew. Ahead of them they could see the snow lying

5

thick on the mountain passes through which they would have to climb, without food or fuel or rest, and with the terror of the French to urge them on. Disease had come, inevitably, to complete the work so well begun by hunger, exposure, and the sword. The typhus – the Black Death – was in among them, along with dysentery and rheumatism and pneumonia. Men dropped dying in the very middle of the road, to be trodden and spurned by comrades too sick and weary to step out of the way, and whose shoeless feet left blood at every step.

If such were the state of affairs at the head of the column, the condition of the rear can hardly be imagined. Here were the men whose legs had given way beneath them, and who still tried to struggle along on hands and knees. Here were the women and children, left ever farther and farther behind, gazing back apprehensively down the road to see when the dreaded helmets of the French dragoons would appear over the rise. Here were the last few relics of the impedimenta of the army, all that had survived the disaster of Espinosa and the hundred miles of the retreat. The horses were all dead, and the few guns and wagons were being dragged along by dying mules, goaded by the drivers who limped along at their sides. It was bad luck on the sick who fell in the highway incapable of moving, for the gun teams were quite incapable of hauling the guns out of the deep central ruts; they could only go straight on regardless.

If any part of the wretched Spanish Bourbon army could boast esprit de corps and devotion to duty, it was the artillery. The gunners of the few guns which had escaped from Espinosa had no real motive in imperilling their lives in dragging their guns on in this fashion. They knew that if they were to cut the traces and leave their pieces behind no one would ever have the energy to make inquiries into the matter. But either their own natural obstinacy or that ingrained by discipline had caused them to drag the things

6

thus far.

The very last unit in the Spanish column – if we except the dying – was a bigger, heavier, and more imposing gun than the iron six-pounders which led the artillery column. Thirteen feet long it was, and two feet in diameter at the breech, and a foot in diameter at the muzzle. It was an eighteen-pounder bronze gun, of that handsome dark alloy which is still known as 'gunmetal'. Around the vent and forward along the barrel it was ornamented with blazonry and heraldic traceries, beautifully designed, and cast as part of the gun itself; it was evidently a gun which had had a mould made expressly for itself at the time of casting, and had clearly been intended as an ornament for some wealthy noble's castle. Round the muzzle, in boldly raised lettering, was a Latin inscription, a fragment of the liturgy of Nocturne – 'And our mouths shall show forth Thy praise.' The gun must have been one of a pair; its brother must have borne the inscription 'Oh Lord, open Thou our lips', and the two must have stood one each side of the entrance ramp of a castle in the South. When the Spaniards rose against the French invaders, and the nation flew to arms after a French army had been engulfed at Baylen, these two guns must have been taken from their ornamental duties to help eke out the woefully inadequate equipment of the Spanish artillery. The other gun had fallen into French hands at some one or other of the disasters which had befallen Spain when Napoleon in his wrath led the Grand Army across the Pyrenees – at Gamonal, perhaps, or Rio Seco, or Tudela, and was probably relegated again by now to ornamental duties at the Tuileries or at Compiègne, to grace Imperial splendour.

It seemed likely enough that the same fate would overtake its fellow, trailing along at the rear of Blake's defeated army. The dozen mules which were dragging its three tons of weight along the rocky road were in the last stages of exhaustion. To force them to take every single step the drivers had to stick their goads into their raw and bleeding sides; the big lumbering gun only surged forward a yard at a time, and every yard with pain and difficulty, crashing and bumping over the rocks which surfaced the road. They reached a point where all the gradients which they had already climbed up into the mountains were inconsiderable compared with the one which now faced them. It seemed to rise before them like the sides of a house; ahead they could see it at intervals winding up the mountain side, as far as the eye could see through the driving sleet. At every hairpin bend the pull of the long string of mules was necessarily at an angle to the length of the gun, with much consequent wastage of power. The drivers shouted, and stuck their goads into the mules' sides until the blood ran in streams; the gunners toiled at the spokes of the wheels with what feeble strength was left them. The wind shrieked round them, dazing them with its force and with the sleet which it hurled along with it. Then the inevitable occurred. One last spasmodic effort carried one wheel up to the top of the rock which had been impeding it; the mules lunged forward under the goads, and the whole thing tottered and fell over on its side in the midst of the road, dragging the limber over with it, and the wheelers in their traces, and then the pair in front, and so on until half the team was down, while the gun lay, huge and ungainly, on its side with one wheel still rotating slowly.

In this fashion the question was settled for the gunners. It would take hours to put that three tons of bronze on to its wheels again. And the mules were past further effort. Those which had fallen lay quietly on the rocky road, their only movement being the distressed heaving of their flanks. With most of them no amount of goading or kicking or cursing could get them on their feet again. When a dying mule finds himself lying down he nearly always decides to lie and die quietly, and no stimulus whatever will get him on his feet again to expend his last few breaths in the service of mankind. The wretched animals who were still on their feet huddled together and tried, as well as their traces would allow, to turn their tails to the sleet-laden wind. At any moment the dragoons might appear in pursuit; the gunners had seen them in among the rear-guard once or twice already during the retreat, slashing about with their swords like a schoolboy among thistles. The wind and the cold and fatigue and hunger had left the gunners too dazed for intelligent effort with levers and ramps. They had just sense enough to open the limber and allow its small content of ammunition to cascade into the road, and then, detaching the limber from the gun, they were able to right the former and hitch the last few mules to it. With this light load they were able to struggle forward again up the interminable mountain road, into the fast falling winter night, while the gun still lay grotesquely with one wheel in the air and the dying mules around it, like some fantastic god surrounded by sacrificed animals – a simile which is not so far from the truth.

The Spanish army went on its way, leaving the gun behind it. Thirty thousand men had fought at Espinosa, and twenty thousand had escaped from that disaster. The march through the mountains, and a winter among their desolate slopes, left some eight thousand fever-ridden phantoms alive next spring to appear again in another corner of Spain and to be sacrificed in some further foolish battle. For the French left their retreat unharried from the morning of the day when the gun was abandoned. Not even a French army could penetrate further into that desolate tangle of mountains, with no more motive than the destruction of a beaten enemy; they wheeled aside and marched down into the plains to Madrid.

CHAPTER II

THE MEN of the mountain valleys, the charcoal burners and the miners, found the gun still lying in the road when next they descended to it. They eyed it with curiosity; for familiar though they were with small arms a cannon was a rare sight among those precipices. So far in this lost corner of the Peninsula the war had barely touched them. Indeed, they had suffered more up to now from the depredation of the starving Spaniards than from the French. The sight of the long desolate road, littered with dead men and dead animals and all the pitiful paraphernalia abandoned in a retreat, was their first introduction to the horrors which were to overwhelm Spain during the next four years. They were men of the mountains, not of the towns. The news that the French Emperor had kidnapped their King and had determined on setting his own brother in his place had been slow in reaching them, and these Galician peasantry did not feel the same intense national pride as did the Castilians and the towns-folk. It was the sight of the dead men along the road, and the tales told by the few living stragglers, and the shameful news of Espinosa, which roused them at last to take their part in the national uprising.

In every mountain village the parish priest mounted his mule and rode off to the nearest town for news, and came back with stories of the formation of provincial governments, of decrees of universal military service, of the organization of new armies to take the place of the old. So that when Father Ciro Prieto came riding up the road in reply to a hurried message, and saw the group of peasants round the gun, he reined in and dismounted with a thrill of pleasure. Artillery was rare among the mountains.

'Good morning, children,' said Father Ciro Prieto, shaking his cassock out of the disorder consequent upon riding astride.

'Good morning, Father,' said they respectfully, and waited for him to take charge of operations. He was a little man with sharp grey eyes, and a great snuff-taker, and much respected all round about as a fount of wisdom. Those sharp eyes of his took in the whole story; the wheel-marks in the road, the position of the gun, turned over at a bend, and the dead mules, made it all obvious to him.

'The French are no further off than Camino Reale,' he said. 'The sooner we get this gun into a place of safety the better.'

'Yes, Father, certainly,' said Vigil the woodcutter. 'But how?'

The priest spread his hands.

'I leave that to you, my sons,' he said. 'Use any means you think will serve.'

Father Prieto's worldly wisdom stopped short at the problem of righting three-ton guns, but he was not going to admit it. He sat at the edge of the road holding the reins of the mule and taking snuff, while his parishioners bustled about the task.

At first their efforts were feeble and ill advised. It was hard for them to realize the enormous weight with which they were dealing. Their early pullings and pryings availed them not at all. It was the copper miners among them who initiated the correct method; they were more used to such difficulties. Two woodcutters were despatched to get a couple of big tree branches as levers. When these were brought back there was at last a real promise of progress. A little hole was dug beneath the barrel of the gun, just in front of the swell of the breech, and the end of a lever thrust into it. Then when ten men flung all their weight upon the other end, behold, the gun moved! It stirred a little in the rut in which it had buried itself. Everyone else promptly flung himself upon the lever. It sank under the combined weight, the gun lifted itself a full foot, and then, the lever slipping from under it, it fell with a shattering crash upon the road again.

'Gently, children, gently,' said Father Prieto from the roadside. His life's experience among these wild mountain people had taught him that they needed far more to be restrained from headlong excess of zeal than to be urged on.

'Gently, you fools,' said Comas the miner. 'That is not the way. Listen – oh, Mother of God!'

Already the wild enthusiasts had pushed the lever under the gun again and were swinging on to it.

'Listen to Andres,' said Father Prieto, sharply, and his flock ceased their heavings while Comas gave a hurried lecture on the use of alternating levers. This time when the gun was heaved up out of its bed Comas was ready. He pushed the second lever under the gun, and a rock beneath it as a fulcrum, and in response to his shouts half the party now flung themselves upon the second lever. The gun rose farther still – Andres' wild exhortations, backed up by Father Prieto, just sufficed to stop them overdoing it again. While the gun hung precariously on the tip of the lever Comas built yet a higher fulcrum, rested the first lever upon it, thrust the lever under the gun, and called to the others to heave again. In this fashion the gun rose steadily, turning over with its carriage to an upright position. There was a tense moment when the rim of the lower wheel took the ground and the gun began to rise upon it. Comas imperilled his life by rushing beneath the swaying mass to pile rocks against the wheel rim when it threatened to slip. As the fulcrums grew higher and higher the effort of turning the gun grew greater and greater; to the very end success hovered in the balance. Just before the gun was ready to fall into the upright position it seemed as if they would never be able to lift it the last necessary six inches. Everyone piled upon the lever, their feet seeking out some grip which might increase their weight; they tugged and they strained, their joints cracking and the sweat running in streams in the cold mountain air. At last Father Prieto left his mule by the roadside and ran to the lever. He found a foot of it unoccupied, grasped it, and lifted his feet from the ground, his legs kicking absurdly within his cassock. His little additional weight turned the scale. The gun swung over, falling with a crash upon its other wheel, tottered, and kept its position, on its two wheels again, pointing with defiance down the road towards the French while the lever, slipping from beneath it, deposited the whole mass of mountaineers in an ungraceful heap on the road.

Everybody rose, panting and full of pride. They swarmed about the gun, examining it with curiosity. They plied Father Prieto with questions about it, most of which the poor man was quite unable to answer. The minute education of a Spanish parish priest did not extend to a knowledge of siege artillery. He could tell them nothing about the employment of the elevating screw and wedge beneath the breech, but he could at least read out the legend round the muzzle – they heard the Latin words with a respectful intake of breath – and translate it for them – 'And our mouths shall show forth Thy praise' – and he found the touch-hole for them (the gun did not boast the elaborate firing arrangements with lock and lanyard which modern artillery possessed) and was able to explain how to load and fire. His flock could understand that; it was just the same simple method as they used in their own muskets, and Father Prieto's economic use of the little knowledge he possessed quite concealed from them his complete ignorance of anything like laying and elevating an eighteen-pounder. They were quite enthralled by his little lecture. Diego Cabrera picked up one of the half-dozen rusty cannon balls which the gunners had spilt from the limber, and weighed it in his hands. Everyone looked longingly at everyone else. The thought was in the minds of all, big children that they were, that it would be fine to load the gun and fire it off, just once. But they looked at the width of the bore and at the cavernous depths of the barrel. A single charge for the monster would consume as much powder as the whole community possessed. Diego let the cannon ball fall reluctantly from his hands.

'Now, into a place of safety with it, children,' said Father Prieto.

That started a new discussion. Anyone could guess that an enormous team would be necessary to drag the gun up the moutain side. Although these peasantry were ready enough to risk their lives, they were all of them peculiarly unwilling to risk their cattle. Horses and mules and draught oxen had been hurried away along with the flocks and herds into safe recesses of the upper valleys even before there was fear of the French coming – the unpaid Spanish armies were just as careless about the rights of property. But no one could disclaim the possession of draught animals to neighbours who knew every detail of his affairs, whatever tales he was willing to tell to commissaries and tax gatherers. Each in turn was gradually provoked into offering the use of a mule or a yoke of oxen, and at last there was a general dispersion to assemble a team, while the few unpropertied men remained behind with the gun, fingering the relief work along its barrel, peeping into the muzzle to see the tiny bit of light which crept in through the touch-hole, passing wise comment on the solidity of the carriage work, while all the time the gun, huge and impassive, stood glaring defiantly down the mountain side. It was well that the French made no move.

Then when the team was got together, in the late afternoon, and harness had been devised, a new difficulty arose. They began by attaching the traces to the iron loop at the tip of the trail of the gun, and found that thus it was impossible to pull the thing along. The trail was devised for limiting recoil, and simply dug itself into the ground when they applied any pull. Clearly the trail must be lifted, and the muzzle depressed, and the gun drawn along in that position. But no cattle on earth were strong enough to maintain sufficient tension on the traces to hold the ponderous weight of the trail in the air. Even Clemente Cagorno's renowned yoke of draught oxen, weighing a ton and a half between them, were dragged backwards as though they had been no more than a pair of nannygoats, while the trail sank back to the ground.

A stray memory came into Father Prieto's mind at last, illuminating it like day. It was a memory ten years old, of an occasion when he had ridden into Burgos, an enormous journey, to consult with the Bishop's secretary. In Burgos he had seen an army on the march, on its way to the Pyrenees to fight the French, who were then red revolutionaries instead of Imperial king makers. There had been guns with that army, clattering through Burgos, and by an excruciating effort Father Prieto remembered how they had been pulled along. The trails of the guns had been swung from limbers – stout two-wheeled carts, to which the horses were harnessed.

With dignity Father Prieto intervened in his parishioners' despairing discussion and explained how the thing should be done, and everyone instantly saw the soundness of the advice. And at the same time everyone – save one – instantly decided who should supply the cart which would take the place of the limber. Isidoro Botto had been the least helpful of any of the group. He had not done much in the matter of righting the gun, and his contribution to the team had been only one unhappy ass, which everyone knew to be sixteen years old if a day. Yet he was the wealthiest of them all, and they knew he owned just the right cart for the business. Each solid pair of wheels was of one piece with the six-inch axles, and they were attached to the wooden cheek pieces with iron staples of best Galician smiths' work, and every bit of wood was of solid Spanish oak. A clamour arose for Botto to offer his cart. He demurred; it was unsuitable for the job in hand; it was out of repair; he had lent it last week to a man from the Asturias; he could not afford to be without it. But he swallowed his objections when Diego Cabrera drew his knife and was imitated by half a dozen others. He went sullenly off with them to his farm to fetch the cart.

It was nearly nightfall when they returned, and humorists declared they could still hear Granny Botto's imprecations, which she had hurled at them when she saw that beloved cart being commandeered, and was presumably still continuing to hurl, some four miles away.

And now the trail of the gun was swung up and fastened to the back axle of the cart, and the motley team was harnessed up. Those who had whips cracked them joyfully; those who had goads plied them with a will, and those with neither ran up and down shouting encouragement. Cart and gun lurched, heaved, and then unmistakably got under way. The difficult corner was rounded, and they set themselves to the climb. Lanterns made their appearance from here and from there, and by their light each successive hairpin bend was negotiated, and the rising of the moon found them over the shoulder of the mountain. Then everyone decided they had done enough for that day.

The further progress of the gun into the heart of the mountains can hardly be followed in so much detail. Certainly it was the very next day that the would-be gunners discovered a truth which the artillery teamster learns speedily enough – that going downhill is more difficult even than going uphill. Three tons of solid metal on a steep slope constitutes a Juggernaut which exacts a cruel toll of lives and broken limbs. The first runaway was only terminated by a crash into the ditch at a bend, with half the team disabled, and incredible labour necessitated in the way of building ramps and working with levers to get the thing on the road again. If the wheels were locked for a descent they ploughed so deep into the road that it was necessary to dig them out again. And if the strain on the ropes which locked the wheels rose above breaking point so that one wheel was suddenly released, that meant another capsizing and more heartbreaking toil to right the gun. Diego Cabrera and Clemente Cagorno and the others came to hate the huge thing which had taken possession of their lives. Isidoro Botto watched with dismay the gradual disintegration of his beloved cart under the shocks and strains to which it was subjected.

But there was some compensation in the fact that the passage of the gun through the mountain villages excited enormous attention. Men who were still hesitating to take up arms were carried away by the spectacle and attached themselves to the party, which increased in snowball fashion. To those unsophisticated mountaineers a force of a thousand peasants with an eighteen-pounder appeared an irresistible army. Father Prieto, rather to his dismay, found himself at the head of one of the most considerable forces of the province, and in consequence a man of weight in the councils of the Junta when the point of concentration was at last reached.

It was one of Fate's bitter ironies that not one of these men who had toiled so Homerically to bear the gun on its way was to see it in action. For more news reached the Junta. The tide of war had oscillated violently back and forth across the Peninsula. Madrid had fallen to the French despite all the boastings of the government. Moore and the English had struck their blow, and had marched the length and breadth of Spain pursued by treble numbers, even along a part of the very road where the gun had been abandoned. Now Moore's army had taken ship at Corunna, leaving their beloved leader buried in the ramparts, and the rumour sped round the countryside that their baulked pursuers were to plunge on through Galicia to complete the conquest of the country. Every available man must be marched by the quickest route to head them off. Father Prieto's Galician band must come, of course. With any luck Soult might be completely surrounded and compelled to surrender, which would bring more glory to Galicia than Baylen did to Andalusia. The gun could not accompany them, however. The route would be by mountain paths, and their experience even on roads had shown how slow was the movement of an eighteen-pounder. Every moment was precious when resounding victory was so near their grasp. The gun must be left, and the men must march at once.

To Father Prieto's credit he improved on the hot-headed Junta's instructions. Perhaps he may have foreseen disaster. The gun was not left standing, as the Junta's orders would have had it, in the street of the little village where they found themselves at the moment. It made one more journey, to where a quarry, unworked now in these turbulent times, had been hacked out of the side of a hill at the edge of the road. The gun was hauled into the basin of the quarry, and lumps of stone were heaped on and around it until a cairn was formed over it. No one would ever suspect that a siege gun was concealed within that mass of stones; the passer-by would naturally assume that the latter was a pile formed during the working of the quarry.

And having completed this good piece of work for Spain Father Prieto and his men marched on to the promised surrounding and destruction of Soult. Of course that promise was not fulfilled. Soult and his veterans of the Grand Army tore their way through the flimsy lines of armed peasants. They rubbed in their easy victories by shooting or hanging or dropping over precipices the prisoners they caught – as indeed they were authorized to do by the laws of war, because their opponents wore no uniform. Father Prieto, poor little man, they hanged in the market square of Vigo because it was well to make a special example of priests, and most of his followers who did not die by violence died by disease. Only a few crept back to their farms and forests among the mountains to try and eke out a living from what was left to them after the exactions of Spanish irregulars and French armies had been met. The gun stayed where it was, hidden in its cairn of stones, month after month, until two years of the interminable war had gone by. French armies came and went; more than once they passed actually beside the gun without discovering it, on their occasional expeditions into the mountain country in pursuit of what they called brigands and the Spanish called guerilleros.

CHAPTER III

AT THE END of that period of two years a man stood on the southernmost ridge of the Cantabrian mountains gazing down into the fertile plain of Leon. The contrast between the scenery close about him and that on the horizon was astonishing. The Cantabrian sierras are formed of row on row of mountain chains, each roughly parallel to the southern coast of the Bay of Biscay, each rocky, steep, and scarped, clothed with forests for most of their height, and their summits nothing more than jagged peaks of naked rock. They are pierced by few paths and by fewer roads, although here and there they enclose rich upland valleys.

But at the very foot of the escarpment above which the man stood gazing down began the plainland, the 'tierra de campos', the 'land of fields', the richest portion of all Spain. Here, as far as the eye could see, stretched rolling cornfields, unbroken by hedges, with hardly a tree to diversify the scene. There were numerous roads which formed a network of yellow streaks over the surface, and which connected the villages which dotted the plain – clusters of one-storeyed cottages, for the most part constructed of sun-dried bricks, whitewashed. There were no rivers to be seen, but the man gazing down from the sierra knew that there were many, that the plain was one of the few Spanish plateaux rich in water. For the rivers had cut themselves beds far below the level of the plain, and flowed at the bottom of deep-sunk ravines, so that only a very keen eye could discern from the mountain top the dark marking of the cañons as they wound about through the folds of the plain. The best way of ascertaining their course, in fact, was to note the little white bridges at the points where the rivers were crossed by the country roads.

The man who stood on the sierra looking over the plain was a guerillero chief, whom his followers knew as 'El Bilbanito', 'the young man from Bilbao'. The Spanish habit of conferring nicknames on anyone of note, from kings to bull-fighters, was specially in evidence in the case of the guerillero leaders. There were the 'Empecinado' – the 'swarthy one' – the 'Cura' – the 'priest' – and the 'Marquesito' – the 'little marquis' – and a hundred others. Between them they were teaching a new lesson in war to the Napoleonic armies who had themselves taught so many to the rest of the world. Unstable and fickle and wayward as they were, the Spanish irregulars were never discouraged, never wholly put down, and were always ready for some new raid on a vulnerable point in the widespread French army of occupation.

El Bilbanito, looking out over the plains as he had looked scores of times before, had an additional motive today for longing to strike a new blow. His forces had just received a most irritating and annoying defeat of a kind to which they were unaccustomed. Two companies of French infantry, marching by night from the plain, had attacked them at dawn after scaling a path which el Bilbanito had been quite certain was unknown to anyone in the French army. There had been a few casualties, although most of the men made their escape easily enough over the face of a precipice and through forest paths where the French had not dared to follow, but what was more exasperating was the loss of everything the band possessed save what was on their persons. Half a dozen pack mules had fallen into the hands of the French, all they had save one, and after two years of war a pack mule was worth its weight in gold. With them had been taken five hundred-weight of powder, quantities of cartridges, some salt meat and biscuits, and much of the treasure which had been accumulated by much harrying of Frenchmen who had already harried Spaniards. The band was sorely annoyed and el Bilbanito's position was badly undermined; indeed had not Pablo, the ambitious second in command, been killed in the fray by a stray bullet (which might possibly have been fired from el Bilbanito's musket) he might have been already deposed. The need to achieve some striking feat of arms was therefore all the more pressing.

Yet by itself the sight of those rich plains was enough to rouse el Bilbanito's zeal. For two years now French garrisons had held those plains, plundering them only moderately, growing fat on their ample products, and with their dominion hardly challenged. No Spanish force could face the French on those plains, for the French possessed discipline, artillery, and cavalry, in all of which the Spaniards were conspicuously lacking. Not even a raid could be attempted on account of those cursed rivers. At every strategic point – which in the plains meant at every river crossing – the French had set down a small sedentary garrison, established sometimes in some strong isolated building or in fieldworks built for the purpose – some of them were visible to el Bilbanito's keen eye. That did not in itself stop raids, for a small party could cross the rivers anywhere, by night if necessary. But sooner or later that small party would encounter a superior force and would have to retreat. And what then? There could be no crossing of those difficult ravines when closely pursued, probably by the dreaded dragoons. They would be hemmed in, taken, and hanged for certain. Before they could run that risk they must make sure of a line of retreat, and to do that they must hold the bridges, and to do that they must capture the covering works. And to do that they must have artillery, which no guerillero band possessed, or could possess, considering the hunted life they led among the mountains.

El Bilbanito followed up this train of thought for the hundredth time, and for the hundredth time came to the same exasperated conclusion. The thing could not be done, although its desirability was so apparent. He stamped with vexation as he turned away from his viewpoint, and walked back along the ridge, over the perfect green turf which the abundant Cantabrian rains caused to grow here, halfway up the mountain side. He was a picturesque enough figure in his loose black trousers, and his red sash with the pistols and the knives in it, and his blouse with the big gilt buttons, and his flowing black cloak buttoned at the neck and billowing out behind him with the speed of his step.

A quarter of a mile along the ridge there was a narrow neck which joined this outpost of the mountains to the main mass of the sierras. At each side here a steep path ran down into the plains, and, uniting, continued along the neck and steeply upwards to the forest-clad slopes. Here, as was to be expected, a sentry was posted, keeping watch along the protruding ridge and down both paths. He stood aside for el Bilbanito, but with small enough respect, so that el Bilbanito watched him out of the corner of his eye as he went by, and felt a creeping of the skin over his spine as he went on up the path lest a shot in the back should end his career then and there. Something would have to be done to keep these mutinous dogs busy.

The path plunged into the pine forest, rising sharply all the time, and only when he had turned a corner among the trees out of sight did el Bilbanito breathe more freely again. His sense of his own dignity had withheld him from looking back. Deep in the forest at a dividing of the ways was another sentry, who displayed a little more deference.

'Jorge has returned, captain,' he said as el Bilbanito went by.

El Bilbanito's only reply was a growl which might have meant anything, but he quickened his step until he reached the clearing which was his temporary head-quarters. Of the hundred men of his band the one or two energetic ones were busied making themselves little huts of pine branches. Half a dozen more were occupied at the fires; apparently Jorge had brought back food from his raid into the mountain village. Perhaps fifty, wrapped in their cloaks, were stretched out here and there in the clearing indulging in their siesta; the rest were sitting idly about awaiting his arrival.

As he made his appearance one of these men arose and came to meet him; it was Jorge, the big smiling boy from the Rioja, who was tacitly assumed to have taken the lately deceased Pablo's place as second in command and was naturally suspected of having designs on that of el Bilbanito himself.

'We have laid our hands on the criminal, captain,' said Jorge with his usual grin.

'Which one?' snapped el Bilbanito.

'The one who caused us to be attacked last week. He is here, captain.'

El Bilbanito brushed Jorge aside and walked over to the seated group.

'He has confessed already, captain,' said Jorge, hurrying after him.

'Why did you not hang him at once, then?' demanded el Bilbanito.

'Because —' but Jorge's explanation was cut short when el Bilbanito reached the group round the prisoner.

It was Isidoro Botto. The loss of his fine cart had been the first step towards a poverty he could not bear; two years of war had stripped him of the possessions of which he had once been so proud. One of Bonnet's infantry columns, marching through the mountains, had stripped his fields of their crops; Frenchmen and Spaniards between them had commandeered his cattle, his barn had been burned, and Botto was now on the point of starvation, just as were most of his compatriots in the debatable land which could be reached but not occupied by French armies. And his brief experience of soldiering when Soult invaded Galicia had quite cured him of any tastes in that direction.

His brown cloth clothes were in rags, but that might have been the result of the mishandling he had just received from the guerilleros; his hands and his feet were tied, and one eye was closed and blackened by a blow. On el Bilbanito's arrival he scrambled awkwardly to his feet and tried to stumble towards him, but his feet were tied too closely, and he only succeeded in falling on his face amid a roar of laughter from the others. His elbows flapped and his legs kicked absurdly. Someone grabbed his collar and hauled him to his feet.

'You won't hang me, Your Excellency?' he said; there were tears on his cheeks. 'You won't have me hanged?'

'I will,' said el Bilbanito.

'But you can't, you can't,' expostulated Botto. The enormity of such a proceeding seemed to make it an impossibility to his mind, but all the same there were horrid doubts within him.

'I can,' said el Bilbanito.

'Oh, Your Excellency —'

'What is the proof against this man?' asked el Bilbanito of Jorge.

'He was out late a week ago. He must have gone down to the French outposts. He knows the path by which the French came – he used to use it for his sheep. And two days back his mother tried to buy food with this.'

Jorge handed over a silver coin to his captain, who scanned it closely. It was a Saragossa dollar – money struck by the French for use in the occupied districts.

'And anyway,' concluded Jorge, 'he has confessed. He admitted his guilt when we were going to hang him over there.'

Jorge jerked his head to indicate the area where this story begins.

'Yes, it is quite true,' said the tearful Botto. He was hysterical with terror. 'But don't hang me. You will lose if you hang me. I can do it again. I can tell them another path by which they can come by night. And then you can be waiting for them. Your Excellency – señores —'

Botto's hands were tied, and this handicap to his gesticulatory powers combined with his fright to reduce him to silence.

For a moment el Bilbanito was tempted. With his inward eye he could picture the ambush at dawn, the slaughter of the wretched French conscripts, the triumph of the day. But no man could survive two years of guerilla warfare without being able to see the disadvantages of the proposed plan. The employment of double traitors, tempting though it might be at first sight, was fraught with too much danger; no one could be certain on which side the balance of treachery would eventually rest. Moreover, in this special case there were practical difficulties. Half the district knew that the man had been arrested and brought into the guerilla camp; if the French were to hear of it it would either be impossible or dangerous to use him. Moreover, if Botto were given the opportunity of another visit to the French outposts the chances were that he would stay there, and the opportunity would be lost of either using him or hanging him. The man's proposal was absurd.

'No,' said el Bilbanito, turning away.

Botto shrieked with despair.

'Hang him,' said el Bilbanito to Jorge.

Willing hands laid hold of the wretched man. They dragged him screaming to a tree. A boy climbed it eagerly and slung a rope over a bough. They fastened the rope about his neck. Botto, gazing at the sky through the noose, saw, like a drowning man, his past life rising before him, from the peccadilloes of childhood to the horrors of the recent past, to his only experience of fighting at Vigo, to the dragging of the gun through the mountains. That memory gave him a fresh wild hope.

'The cannon!' he shrieked. 'I know where the cannon is.'

El Bilbanito heard the words and turned sharply on his heel. They chimed in so exactly with his thoughts of half an hour ago, when he had been asking himself where he could find artillery. He hurried back just as they swung Botto off his feet, just as the last shriek of 'The cannon!' was cut in half by the tightening noose. At his signal they lowered Botto to the ground again; fortunately the jerk had not broken his neck.

'What was that you said?' demanded el Bilbanito.

Botto tore at the noose with his bound hands; his eyes bulged; even when they loosened the rope he had to gasp and swallow for some minutes before he could speak.

'We buried a cannon,' he said at length. 'A big, big cannon, when I was with Father Prieto. Before you came here, Your Excellency. I am sure no one has found it since.

I am the last of those who were there.'

'Where was it you buried it?'

'Over the mountains, a hundred miles from here. I can take you there, Your Excellency.'

'Where was it?'

'On the side road to Lugo, two villages beyond Monforte. A great big cannon, Your Excellency.'

'In what place did you bury it?'

'In a quarry just outside the village, Your Excellency.'

'H'm,' said el Bilbanito. 'Are there many quarries there?'

'I don't think so, Your Excellency. There will be no difficulty —'

Botto choked anew as he saw the trap into which he had fallen, and he began to beg again for his life.

'Oh, you won't hang me now, Your Excellency?' he screamed. 'You must take me with you to find the cannon. You can hang me if my story is not true. It is true, by all —'

'What else have you to tell me?'

A little spontaneous inventive power might at this moment have saved Botto's life. If he could only, with some verisimilitude, have laid claim to further knowledge, and offered to barter it against a promise of pardon, he might have prolonged his wretched existence, for a space at least. But he was not endowed with creative ability. He had to stop and think, to try to devise something, and el Bilbanito, watching him closely through his narrowed eyes, saw the truth, saw that no further useful revelations were to be expected.

'Bah!' he said, and he called to the men who still held the rope: 'Up with him.'

It was only five minutes more of life that Botto had gained for himself, and the five minutes were now ended.

El Bilbanito was grimly satisfied with himself as he

walked away. He had a reputation for ferocity to maintain; he hoped the incident had made a suitable impression on his band. It had been rather amusing to have the poor fool blab out all he knew and then hang him after all; it would not be difficult to find the gun, in a quarry two villages beyond Monforte on the road to Lugo, without him. And it was just as well the man was dead. That saved a good deal of the possibility that the news that the guerilleros would soon be armed with artillery might leak out to the French – trust a guerilla chief to know the value of surprise. There might be traitors among his own followers, all the same – el Bilbanito's pensive expression hardened, and he put his hand to his pistols at the thought – well, the recent hanging would make them cautious, at any rate.

El Bilbanito's mind went on making plans, devising how he could make best use of this possible gun. It would have to be a hard, sudden stroke. El Bilbanito's motives in making his plans with such care were only very slightly selfish. True, he certainly wished to regain his prestige among his followers. And there was a good deal of the spirit of the true craftsman in wishing to make the best job possible of the work he found to his hand. But also there was Spanish patriotism within him, a hatred of the French invader, a desire to bring back the king whom the French had kidnapped, a passionate resentment against the nation which had meddled so gratuitously with Spanish affairs, a longing for revenge upon the enemy who had brought such calamities upon the country. Spanish pride and Spanish patriotism were in this case working hand in hand with the instinct of self-preservation.

El Bilbanito's decision was reached quickly enough. He signalled to Jorge.

'Call the men together,' he said, curtly. 'We march in ten minutes.'

That was all the order necessary in a guerilla band.

They marched with all they had, and they were unused to having explanations offered them by their high-handed leaders.

CHAPTER IV

THE ROUTE which el Bilbanito's Cantabrian band had to follow was complicated by the fact that most of the main passes in the Asturias and in part of Galicia were commanded by French garrisons, but el Bilbanito was perfectly capable of devising a route which would steer clear of them, and that without a map and without a moment's reflection. Two years of guerilla warfare had taught him every mountain path in the province; at any moment he could say instantly which passes were likely to be blocked with snow, and which fords impassable with floods, according to the season. That kind of knowledge was part of his stock in trade; it was in consequence of it that he was able (on most occasions, at least) to elude the pursuit of the French columns which were sent after him on the rare occasions when the garrisons of the plains were able to scrape together a surplus of men for the purpose.

There were moments during the march when his heart misgave him slightly. If the expedition were to prove a wild goose chase his men were likely to get out of hand. The possibility had to be faced, but he had encountered mutiny before and the likelihood did not worry him unduly; he only saw to it that his pistols were invariably primed and loaded. If he wanted the gun there was no other course open to him than the one he was following. Had he merely sent a small party to find if the gun were there he knew perfectly well that before he could bring it up to join him it would be commandeered by some other band or by the hunted group of refugees who called themselves the Galician junta, and if he went for it himself he would not only meet the same difficulty, but his band would elect another leader in his absence. Besides, a hundred miles of rapid marching would do his men good; they were growing fat and lazy and it was important to conserve the incredible marching capacity which they were capable of displaying.

The villagers of Molinos Reales resigned themselves to the inevitable when a new band of guerilleros descended upon them from the mountains. They were used to it by now, and guerilleros were at any rate one degree better than French. El Bilbanito billeted himself on the house of the alcalde, and distributed his men among the stone-built cottages which clustered about the church. Every householder found himself with one or two men to feed and house, and if these men's boots and clothes were worn out, as they mostly were, he had to resign himself to handing over the small contents of his wardrobe to them and donning instead their cast-off rags. The worst of guerilleros was their habit of descending without warning from the hills; if regular troops or French came along there was nearly aways sufficient time to hide what few valuables were left, drive the sheep and cattle into the mountains, and assume an aspect of poverty even more abject than was really the case.

El Bilbanito allowed his men the luxury of twenty-four hours under roofs, with as much food as they could coerce from their unwilling hosts. He himself, with Jorge and two chosen aides-de-camp, went off immediately to the quarry which the alcalde indicated to them. The fact that there was such a quarry certainly boded well for the confirmation of the story of the man they had left dangling from a pine tree on the borders of Leon. And the basin of the quarry was level with the road, surrounded only on three sides by the steep-cut sides – a further indication of probability. And there, in the centre of the basin, there was a huge pile of broken stone, which must have been there some time because two or three blades of grass were growing on it.

With a little feeling of excitement el Bilbanito pulled a stone or two from the heap, and then, remembering his dignity, desisted.

'Pull that heap down,' he said to his followers, and, turning his back, he strolled away with a magnificent assumption of indifference.

He heard the clatter and rattle of the stones as Jorge and the others set to work, and when he heard their cry of delight he turned hastily back and rejoined them. The gun was there, surely enough. Already its huge long barrel was visible above the dwindling pile, and they were digging away the stones from about its carriage.

El Bilbanito examined it carefully. Its metal had assumed a dull green colour with all the moisture to which it had been exposed, but that was a reassuring sign. It proved that the gun was of bronze, and bronze will endure centuries of exposure; an iron gun would be honeycombed with rust by now. Indeed, the ironwork of the mounting, the screw controlling the wedge below the breech, the staples of the carriage, the rims of the wheels, were red and rotten and crumbling. Even the stout oak and chestnut of the carriage had suffered. Lichens had grown up on them. But the gun itself, the irreplaceable, was intact. El Bilbanito ran his fingers with joy over the relief work along the barrel, and slapped its fat trunnions, and with the needle that his dandyism caused him always to carry he dug the dirt out of the touch-hole. Then he hastened back to the village.

The alcalde was confronted with a demand for carpenters and smiths. He spread his hands deprecatingly. He explained in his barbarous Gallego dialect that skilled workmen of that sort were scarce nowadays. But el Bilbanito would listen to no excuses. The village carpenter

31

was sent for, and within an hour the alcalde, escorted by Jorge and half a dozen men, was on his way over the hills to the next village in search of a smith of repute who was known to live there. El Bilbanito with a working party and the armourer of the band – a gunsmith who had strayed into the band from Aragon – hurried back to the gun.

The armourer knew nothing about artillery, nor did el Bilbanito, but they were men of experience and common sense, of inventive capacity and ingenuity, as befitted survivors of two years of mountain warfare. Men who had bridged crevasses with an enemy in hot pursuit, who could swing loaded mules over precipices and set them unhurt on their feet at the bottom, were not likely to be deterred by the difficulties of handling a three-ton gun. El Bilbanito set his party – partly his own men, partly impressed villagers – to work on the construction of tall shears over the gun. The armourer sketched the elevating apparatus for future reference. The carpenter examined the carriage, noting measurements and dimensions; as he could neither read nor write he had to notch them cabalistically on pieces of wood, but he was used to doing his work like that.

Plans were complete by the time Jorge returned with both a smith and carpenter whom he had torn from their homes with the comforting assurance that it would not be more than a week or two before they would be allowed to return. The armourer was already improvising a forge, and a detachment detailed by el Bilbanito was conducting a house to house search for all the iron which could be discovered, brazeros and such-like. By the next morning the smiths and carpenters between them had constructed the necessary pulley blocks, the shears were reared over the gun, and el Bilbanito was anxiously supervising the swinging of the vast mass of metal cut out of its carriage.

Jorge selected, with the aid of the carpenter, the best

pieces of weathered oak from the latter's stock. Jorge knew nothing about timber, but, as he explained with his eternal grin, he made sure of getting the best and most valuable pieces by simply insisting on taking those which the carpenter was most voluble in explaining would not do.

The gun swung in its slings over its carriage. Thanks to the quadruple pulleys in the blocks a dozen men had sufficed to lift it far enough for the trunnions to clear the deep notches in which they rested. The wreck of the carriage was run from beneath it, and then, ever so carefully – el Bilbanito would have shot the man who was clumsy – the huge thing was lowered to the ground, and el Bilbanito turned his attention to urging on the smiths and the carpenters to complete their work of fashioning a new carriage.

The man was in a fever of excitement. He knew, even better than unfortunate Father Prieto had suspected two years before, what prestige the possession of artillery would bring him among the guerilleros of the province. But more than that, he carried in his mind's eye that mental picture of the fat plains, and the helpless garrisons dotted over them – helpless, that is to say, in face of an eighteen-pounder – and the ruin he could wreak upon the long vulnerable lines of communication stretching far to the rear of the French armies in the field.

All day long and for days afterwards the little village rang with the beat of the hammers on the extemporised anvils. There were iron rims to be made, fitting so exactly the broad wooden wheels which the carpenters were making that only when they were strongly heated would they slip over the felloes, so that when they were cool they would hold the wheels together despite the strain to which they were to be subjected. The screw handle which forced in and out the elevating wedge beneath the breech had to be painfully forged by hand out of bar iron, and, more difficult still, the threaded sockets in which it had to revolve. Axle pins and so forth were easy enough – the Galician smith had passed his days on that sort of work.

Even el Bilbanito had to grant an occasional rest to the weary ironworkers. He chafed at their taking six hours for sleep, but he allowed them to do so each night. He confiscated for them the best of wine and provender, and he sent his detachments far and wide to secure for them a sufficiency of charcoal. In four days the work was completed – a perfect new carriage was made for the gun. Perhaps it was not quite so prepossessing in appearance as the old one had been at its best, but it was a wonderful piece of work. The cheeks, on which the trunnions were to rest, were of four-inch oak, and the notches themselves were faced with beech. The axle was of oak too, six inches in diameter. The spokes of the wheels were of the finest ash that could be found; those wheels were the wonder of a district which had never seen other than plain solid discs cut from trees. El Bilbanito grudgingly gave his approval when he came to inspect it finally, but he reserved his final decision until a trial should be made.

The carriage was run out to the quarry, the gun slung up again by the shears, and the carriage pushed beneath it. Then the gun was slowly lowered into position, with the armourer rushing back and forth to see that it was properly done. Slowly the trunnions entered into the sockets, and bedded themselves down. The vast breech settled itself upon its block, and the sling rope slacked off as the carriage took the strain. The woodwork creaked at the first imposition of its three-ton burden, but everything held firm. The armourer clamped down the iron holdfasts over the notches, and passed on to examine the rest. Everything was perfect. Zero on the newly forged scale exactly corresponded with the groove on the gun's breech – or within a quarter of an inch, which was good enough for siege artillery work. The trunnions fitted the sockets exactly; there was no trace of rocking or rolling. When the elevating screw was wound out the wedge below the breech slid sweetly backwards, and the muzzle of the gun rose steadily, and the notch on the breech moved regularly down the ranging scale. The gun, so the armourer declared, was ready to work, and el Bilbanito issued his order to prepare it for firing.

The armourer was delighted; it would be a further opportunity of demonstrating his attention to detail and anticipation of instructions. One of the two reserve powder kegs was brought up and opened. A liberal measure of powder was scooped up and poured into the muzzle of the gun, a rammer which the armourer had prepared of a bundle of rags on the end of a pole was pushed up the barrel so that all the powder was packed into the breech, and then a piece of blanket was stuffed up after it to hold it firm. Next the armourer produced his masterpiece – a big round boulder selected from the bed of a stream and bound round with leather so as to fit the bore of the gun. This was pushed in on top of the wadding, and the gun was loaded.

At the armourer's order half a dozen men laid hold of the trail, two others worked with levers at the wheels, and the gun was swung round until it pointed out of the quarry, across the road. The armourer mounted on the trail and fussed with the laying screw – which gave the necessary amount of fine adjustment in the lateral aiming of the gun which mere pulling round of the gun and carriage could not give with certainty. Looking through the notch on the bar of the backsight he had made yesterday, the armourer aligned the groove on the muzzle swell with a patch of white rock showing up through the undergrowth of the mountain side across the valley. Then he turned the elevating screw until the mark on the breech corresponded with the figure '250' on the elevation scale. The armourer had never in his life fired at such a range as two hundred and fifty varas, not even with the long Tyrolese rifle his lordship the Marquis of Lazan had brought him to repair before the war, but he estimated the distance as well as he could by the light of Nature. Next he scooped a little more powder from the keg, and with it filled the touch-hole. Last of all he produced flint and steel and tinder, caught, after many attempts, a spark upon this last, and transferred it to a length of slow match which he blew into a glow. All excitement, he was about to lay the match on the touch-hole when the harsh voice of el Bilbanito called him back. He was not to be the man to fire the first shot from the gun.

El Bilbanito took the match, hardly hearing the armourer's pattered instructions. He had sense enough without them to stand clear of the wheel in the recoil, and he knew well enough that the way to fire a gun was to apply a match to the touch-hole. Leaning far over, he pressed the spark against the loose grains of powder visible round the edge. There was a sharp fizzling noise, instantly drowned in an immense, a gigantic bellowing explosion. The enormous volume of the noise quite dazed el Bilbanito; it was much bigger than he had expected. The gun rushed from beside him in its recoil, crushing the fragments of rock beneath its wheels, and a huge cloud of smoke enveloped him. Through the smoke he could hear a wild cheer from his men.

Then the smoke cleared away. He was still standing holding the smouldering match, and the gun was four yards away. His men were gesticulating and pointing, and, looking in the direction they indicated, he saw that a little cloud of dust still hung over the patch of rock at which the gun had been aimed. The armourer had indeed achieved a miracle.

And the gun stood there with a faint wisp of smoke still trickling from its muzzle, immense, imposing, huge. It almost looked as if it were filled with contempt for the little marionettes of men who capered round it, little things whose lives could be measured, at the best, in scores of years, and who were quite incapable unaided of hurling death across five hundred yards of valley.

CHAPTER V

IT WAS not until the gun had been tried and proved that el Bilbanito allowed himself to send out the letters he had looked forward so eagerly to dispatching. Haughty letters they were, as befitted the only chieftain in Galicia who possessed an eighteen-pounder. All save one were addressed to the other guerillero leaders in this debatable land. They announced the brief fact that el Bilbanito now disposed of siege artillery and was intending an attack upon Leon; anyone who cared to come and serve under him would be welcomed. That the offer would be eagerly accepted el Bilbanito had not the least doubt; no one could lead the life of a guerillero and not yearn to push down into the plains; so great would be the desire that the chiefs would swallow their pride and consent to act as his subordinates – or, if they did not, their men would desert and flock to join the leader who could offer them with so much certainty plunder and victory beyond anything achieved up to now.

The other letter was just as peremptory and was addressed to the Junta – the hunted local government – of Galicia. It, too, announced that el Bilbanito now owned a gun, and it demanded instant supplies of powder and eighteen-pound shot, with plenty of pack animals to carry them, and ample forage, and muleteers. As an afterthought el Bilbanito included in his comprehensive demands a request for money, food, and clothing – not that he particularly hoped to get them, but because there was a faint

37

chance that the Junta might have some stores for once in a way, and he felt he was just as entitled to a share as anyone else.

While he was awaiting answers to all his letters el Bilbanito took in hand the business of getting the gun back over to the edge of the plains. All the energy which Father Prieto and his party had expended in carrying the gun so far was not merely wasted, but was the source of a great deal of trouble, for el Bilbanito wished to bring the gun into action not many miles from the point where its regular gunners had abandoned it. And there was the question now of those French posts on the high road through the mountains; they would have to be circumvented. The gun would have to return by the route which el Bilbanito and his men had followed – over the crests, by the footpaths. The alternative was to use the gun to help storm the French posts, and from that el Bilbanito turned resolutely away. When he struck, he wished to strike at the heart; the reduction of the mountain garrisons would take time, and the plainlands would receive warning before he could be in among them.

Far and wide el Bilbanito sent his men in search of draught animals. They were hard to get nowadays. In one village where he came in person and demanded oxen the priest took him and, pointing down the valley, showed him a plough being dragged over a field by a strange team indeed – a little white ass, a man, and four women, the human beings bent double with the strain and only preserving their balance by supporting themselves on their hands, while an old white-haired man exerted his feeble strength at the handles. El Bilbanito laughed and took the ass, and the women were white to the lips as they saw him and his men go off with it. Spring was near at hand, the ploughing was not a quarter finished, and they would starve before the year was out.

The asses and the one mule and the six oxen they collected at last served their purpose in getting the gun under way. Two wheels on an axle served as a limber to which to attach the trail, and for some miles the gun moved nobly along the high road. But soon they reached the point where a footpath came down the mountain side and joined the road. It was up this path that the gun had to go. El Bilbanito had ordered it, and he was here with his pistols to see that it was done. A mass of rocks was carried down to bridge the ditch. The motley string of animals struggled over it, the gun crashed after them, and the struggle began.

These lower crests of the Cantabrian mountains, on the borders of Galicia and Asturias, are covered with that dense growth of spiny bushes which is best known to English people by its Corsican name of 'maquis', but which the Galician peasant calls the 'monte bajo' – an impenetrable tangle of small evergreen trees of different species, growing precariously on the rocky slopes. The mountain side, too, is not a continuous uphill, but is broken up into a precipitous switchback with a general upward tendency, but alternated with down slopes as steep as the roof of a house.

Ten men went on ahead with axes, cutting the undergrowth at each side of the path to allow the animals following them to push along it two abreast. Beside the team walked the drivers, one man to each animal, with whips and goads, ready at a shout from el Bilbanito in the rear to stimulate their charges into fresh frantic efforts. Forty men walked beside the gun and limber, distributed along the trail ropes; they had to be ready to pull forward or back, or to turn the gun round corners, as the difficulties of the path dictated. Then came a dozen men carrying two thick trunks of trees, and ready to drop these behind or in front of the wheels to act as 'scotches' where necessary.

It was el Bilbanito's personality which carried the gun over those mountains. His men would soon have abandoned the task as hopeless, despite the assistance which their leader got for them by conscripting the aid of all the peasants, men and women, whom he could catch. There were times when an hour's labour meant only ten yards of progress. That was up the steeper inclines, when they had first to disperse and gather small rocks to make some sort of road surface, and long ramps up and down at points where the path charged over some steep minor ridge of rock at gradients which would compel a man to go on hands and knees. On these steep slopes men and animals would rest to get their breath, while the gun was held up by the scotches, until a warning shout from el Bilbanito caused the men at the drag ropes to take the strain again, and the drivers to hitch their goads ready in their hands. Then el Bilbanito would shout 'Pull!' and the men would tug, and the whips would crack, and the animals would tug and flounder about on the uncertain foothold, and the gun would move ever so little – a yard or two at most – up the slope before the effort died away and the scotches were dropped hastily behind the wheels again and the gasping beasts of burden – on two legs or on four – could rest again.

The animals would fall and break their legs between rocks, but others could be got as the party moved on; a peasant threatened instant death would generally reveal where an ass or an ox could be found. There was rarely any need to apply torture. Even cows had to be used – to this day the Galicians and Asturians use cows for draught purposes – but cows, with all the contrariness of their sex, persisted in dying under the strain without even the excuse of broken bones. The men did not die. They cursed el Bilbanito, they cursed the gun, and the cattle, but they lived. During this period el Bilbanito slept more securely than before; he knew that mutiny breeds in idleness, not in hardship or hard work. The men might curse, complain, grumble, but they were secretly proud of their efforts. There was a thrill in looking back down a seemingly endless mountain side and in knowing that they had dragged a gun all the way up it. Unremitting toil of the most exacting nature had always been the destiny of those peasants even in peace time, and now in war their labour was made more attractive for them because each man wore a plume of cock's feathers in his hat and belonged to the noted guerillero band of el Bilbanito, which was soon to sweep the plains of Leon by the aid of the gun.

In the mountains above Bembibre they found the first results of the letter writing el Bilbanito had done before setting out. As they came lumbering down into a village a band of ragged guerilleros came forth to welcome them from the houses in which they had been billeted. Foremost among them were two men not at all of the Galician type. They were tall and slender, with mobile humorous faces, and both of them had blue eyes and black hair – a most unusual combination. El Bilbanito knew them by reputation. They were the brothers O'Neill, Hugh and Carlos, who at the head of their Asturian band had distinguished themselves the year before when the Spaniards had tried to raise the siege of Astorga. Their surname explained their colouring – they were the descendants of some Irishman, possibly one who had 'left his country for his country's good', or who had joined the Spanish army to avoid the tyranny of Cromwell or of William III a hundred and fifty years ago. Men with Irish names teemed in the Spanish ranks; most of them were more Spanish than the Spaniards by now, and few could speak English.

The two O'Neills bowed to el Bilbanito with much ceremony. They could appreciate what he had achieved in bringing the gun thus far, and they could appreciate still more the advantages the possession of the gun conferred. El Bilbanito, on the other hand, was equally glad to see them. He needed a large force for his projected raid into Leon, and so was glad of the reinforcement; still more was he glad of the promise it held out of further additions to his force.

Carlos O'Neill was clearly all a-bubble with excitement as he stepped up to the gun and examined it.

'My brother was in the artillery once,' expained Hugh to el Bilbanito.

'Indeed?' said the latter, with increasing interest. A trained artillery officer was a most desirable acquisition.

They watched him as he looked over everything, examining the elevating and training gear, the detail of the carriage work, the soundness of the metal of the gun itself. Then he came back to them.

'Well?' asked el Bilbanito; for the life of him he could not keep a trace of anxiety out of his voice.

'May I congratulate you, señor?' said Carlos. 'It is a magnificent weapon. Your Excellency must have good workmen to put together so good a mounting. They were artillerymen, I take it?'

'No,' said el Bilbanito. 'I have none with me.'

'Indeed?' said Carlos in his turn, and the two brothers looked at each other.

'So you expected *us* to supply artillerymen when you wrote and invited us to join you, señor?' said Hugh, haughtily.

El Bilbanito shrugged his shoulders.

'You or the others. It was of no importance to me. I should contrive something, anyway. Call your men out and set them at the drag ropes. Mine are in need of a rest.'

The inevitable quarrel between the chiefs might have flared out there and then. The Spaniard does not assume authority gracefully; he suffers from the defects of his qualities, and becomes overbearing when he finds himself in the position of leader. But at the moment the situation was eased by the rapid fraternization of the two bands. The O'Neills' men had in fact forestalled el Bilbanito's order, and, swarming out of the cottages, had relieved the new arrivals of their duties at the gun. At the moment they were going slightly downhill, and they were on a path which might almost be called a road from its width and regularity, so that the change was effected without difficulty. The two O'Neills had to break off the conversation in order to get their belongings from the house, hurriedly, for fear of being left behind. It was undignified, they felt.

They felt better when they came clattering up on their horses to catch up the column, for el Bilbanito was on foot like the rest of his men, like a true mountaineer. Carlos O'Neill, especially, could look down on el Bilbanito trudging along behind the gun, because his horse was an immense animal, a seventeen-hand grey, a most surprising sight in this land of fine mules and diminutive horses.

'Horses!' said el Bilbanito. 'They will be useful when we leave the road again. Our team is weak, as you see.'

'No, señor,' replied Carlos O'Neill indignantly. 'You will not have Gil to pull in traces. I value him far too much.'

'I shall have him if I think it necessary,' retorted el Bilbanito.

'No, no, no, never,' said Carlos. 'Take your hand away from your pistol, sir!'

El Bilbanito was determined to display his authority, and to nip any incipient rebellion in the bud. But as he drew and cocked his pistol, Hugh O'Neill's riding whip came down on his wrist, and the weapon exploded harmlessly. El Bilbanito flung the empty pistol into Carlos' face.

At the sound of the shot the two bands of men on ahead with the gun stopped and came running back, and the animals, grateful for the rest, began to munch the grass at the roadside. Carlos O'Neill had dismounted, and the big grey horse stood behind him looking over his shoulder like some wise counsellor whispering in his ear.

'You shall die for that blow,' said Carlos, wiping the blood from his cheek. Hugh O'Neill came round beside him; the guerilleros began to draw up on each side of the road, the two bands facing each other. Muskets were being cocked; there seemed every likelihood of a bloody little battle on the spot.

'As you will,' said el Bilbanito. 'Here and now.'

Jorge was at his elbow. Carlos drew his sword.

'Holy Mary, Mother of God!' said Carlos. 'The fellow has no sword!'

'Not I,' said el Bilbanito. 'We settle our quarrels with the knife, we men of the mountains.'

'Do you expect *me*, with the blood of kings in my veins, to fight like a brigand with knives?' demanded Carlos.

'Of course, if you are afraid, señor —' said el Bilbanito.

Carlos looked round him. His ragged Asturians for once had no sympathy with him. They knew nothing of the etiquette of the duel, and they took it for granted that knives should be used; as far as their knowledge went the knife was the national weapon of Spain. El Bilbanito was very sure of his ground.

'It is nothing to me,' said Carlos, his fighting blood aflame. 'Lend me your knife, you.'

Even his brother could not remonstrate. An O'Neill could not be expected to refuse a challenge to fight with any weapon, at any time, against any opponent. All Hugh O'Neill could do was to watch to see that no unfair advantage was taken, and to hold himself ready to challenge el Bilbanito himself if – inconceivably – his brother should be defeated.

The sky was wintry and grey, and a cold wind blew down from the snow-covered peaks which closed in the horizon. At the edge of the road stood the gun, huge and immovable, with the weary animals harnessed to it in a long double line. The guerilleros were ranged in an irregular oblong, enclosing the piece of road where the quarrel was to be fought out, and in an angle of the oblong stood Hugh O'Neill, with the reins of the two horses over his arm; ever and anon he patted Gil's neck to reassure him in this matter of his master. In the middle of the oblong the two men seemed to dance a strange, formal dance. Each held his cloak over his left arm with the end fluttering loose; in his right hand each held a knife, the long, slightly curved weapon of Spain, blade upwards, thumb towards the blade as a knife ought to be held. Each was bent a little at the knees and hips, and taut like a spring. They sidled round each other right-handed, their eyes narrowed with the strain of watching every movement of the enemy. Feint and counter-move followed each other like the steps of the dance which a casual observer might think they were dancing. Here and there in the ranks of the spectators men coughed nervously. In a fight with knives one man must die as soon as the opponents come within arm's length.

El Bilbanito had no fear of the result; he had fought too many of these duels, and, as he would simply say, he had not been killed yet. This man O'Neill handled his knife and cloak like a tyro, and caution was only forced on el Bilbanito on account of O'Neill's long reach and vigilant eyes. Yet they would not save O'Neill, not with el Bilbanito in front of him. If a feint did not throw him off his guard he could goad this beginner into making an attack which would lay him open to a deadly counterstroke. El Bilbanito moved farther to his right, and O'Neill turned to face him. But even while he turned, quick as a flash el Bilbanito leaned to his left and dashed within O'Neill's guard. By a miracle O'Neill caught the knife on his cloak; it went through the cloak and through his arm; with satisfaction el Bilbanito felt the blade jar on the bone. He caught his enemy's right wrist in his left hand, and bent his knees and braced his thick body for the throw which would follow. The fight was won.

Perhaps his grip slipped; perhaps O'Neill's arms were stronger than he expected. O'Neill's wrist slipped from his hand. El Bilbanito was conscious of a violent blow on his side, which deprived him of his breath. There was a sharp

45

pain in his chest, but it soon passed. El Bilbanito never knew that he had lost that fight; he never knew he was dying. With a strange dull curiosity he noticed his knees grow weak under him, and he felt himself, without knowing why, sink slowly on to the stones of the road. The light hurt his eyes, and he turned gently on to his face and lay limp. And over him stood Carlos O'Neill, with the knife in his right hand red to the hilt. El Bilbanito's knife still transfixed his left arm, from which the blood came in spouts, and ran down his wrist and fingers.

CHAPTER VI

THERE WAS Spanish regular infantry in the village which looked out over the plain. They were the Princesa Regiment, but they were not the least like the old regular army, the men who had worn the white Bourbon uniforms, with the cocked hats and the tight breeches and the black gaiters. These men wore the rough brown homespun cloth of the country; the coats were cut away in tails at the back, and the trousers fastened with straps under the foot. And they wore shakoes, too, so that altogether they looked like gross caricatures of English soldiers.

The appearance of caricature went farther than the clothing, for the men were at drill, and drilling grotesquely. The lines were ragged, and there was no attempt at keeping step, and when finally the colonel gave the word to form square there was hesitation, muddle, until in the end the regiment fell together in one vast pudding-like mass, bayonets pointing in all directions, while the colonel and the adjutant raved from their saddles. In despair of ever sorting out the confusion by drill-book methods the colonel called out company markers, and gave the word for the regiment to fall in on them, and while the men slouched to their places the colonel made ready in his mind the speech he determined to deliver, in which he would paint in vivid terms the fate of the Princesa Regiment if ever it tried to form square in that fashion with Kellermann's dragoons charging down upon it.

It was unfortunate that at the moment when the colonel began his lecture there should come distraction from the mountain tops. Over the crest high up on the left a little procession came into view. The men and animals and vehicles composing it were dwarfed to specks by the distance, but in the clear mountain air they could be seen clearly enough, while even the sound of their progress, the shouts of the men leading the team, could be heard as a faint shrill piping. The spectacle was far more interesting than the colonel's hysterical lecture on tactics; every eye was turned up the mountain side, and soon every face was, and then in the end, while the colonel almost wept, the whole regiment broke up and lounged over to watch the fun.

The process of bringing the big gun down the mountain side was really exciting. There were four long drag ropes stretched out behind it, with thirty men to each, and every man lying back taking the strain and only allowing the gun to descend foot by foot to the accompaniment of the directing shouts of the leaders. In front a quaintly assorted team of draught animals was being led down, while round about the gun a dozen wildly energetic men were running back and forth, rolling the bigger rocks out of the way, working like fiends with levers when irregularities of surface tended to tip the gun on its side, and dropping scotches in front of the wheels when the dragrope teams became disorganized and there was a chance that the gun might tear loose and come charging down the mountain on its own. Then when the angle of slope altered and the gun was faced by a short uphill the excitement redoubled. The team had to be harnessed up to the limber, a good momentum imparted, to the accompaniment of deafening yells, to the gun on the last bit of downhill, and then the drag-rope crews had to rush round so as to pull forward instead of back to carry the gun as far as possible up the slope until the momentum died away and spasmodic efforts were substituted for it, each painfully dragging the gun another yard or two up until the next crest was reached. Altogether it was a most entertaining spectacle.

When at last the gun reached the road the regiment eyed it and its escort with curiosity. The gun was huge, enormous, in their eyes, accustomed only to the little field six-pounders which were all the Spanish army could boast nowadays. It came crashing and clattering down the road on its vast five-foot wheels with a most intoxicating noise. The odd team which drew it – three mules, six asses and a couple of cows – did not appear so strange; they were used to seeing the military train drawn by assorted teams. And the men who came with it were not so unusual a spectacle either; they had often seen guerillero bands before, and more than half of them had been guerilleros themselves before they had been caught and clapped into the ranks of the army.

At the head of the band rode a tall young man in a captain's uniform on a small brown horse; beside the gun rode another man in the blue coat of the artillery, much patched and very ragged, and the fact that his left arm was in a sling accounted for his having mounted his horse on the wrong side on reaching the road. His horse seemed to have been proportioned to the gun, so colossal an animal it was, a huge, bony grey like some horse out of a picaresque romance.

The Princesa Regiment witnessed the meeting between the colonel and these two officers, and saw them escorted with much politeness to regimental headquarters beside the village church while the colonel's grooms attended to their horses. And then the regiment found itself, as frequently happens, with nothing to do. The men fraternized with the guerilleros, and examined the big gun with curiosity, and idled about as only Spaniards can, until their idling was interrupted by the sudden appearance of the guerillero captain in the little square outside the church. He clambered on to the breech of the gun, and all through the village they heard him shout, 'Princesa! Princesa!' and they came running to hear what he had to say.

CHAPTER VII

'I AM Colonel de Casariego y Castagnola, of the Princesa Regiment of infantry,' said the colonel, introducing himself, 'and my adjutant, Captain Elizalde.'

'I am Captain Hugh O'Neill, late of the Ultonia Regiment,' said O'Neill. 'May I present my brother, Don Carlos O'Neill, of the Artillery?'

The introductions were almost ceremonious; it was not until they were comfortably seated in headquarters that any topic of business was mentioned.

'I understood from my orders,' said the colonel, 'that a certain el Bilbanito was bringing the gun here.'

'We have el Bilbanito's men with us,' replied Hugh O'Neill, 'but el Bilbanito himself, most unfortunately, did not survive the difficulties of the journey.'

'But how sad,' said the colonel. 'How did he die?'

'It was a sudden indigestion,' interjected Carlos O'Neill.

'Very sudden,' elaborated Hugh.

'I have heard of the disease before,' said the colonel. 'Was it steel or lead he was unable to digest? Or perhaps – perhaps he suddenly found himself unable to breathe?'

'It was something like that,' said Hugh airily.

'Quite so, of course,' said the colonel, with his glance drifting over Carlos O'Neill's bandaged arm. 'And now to business.'

The colonel did not seem in too great a hurry to start, all the same. He took a long pull at his cigar, and he made a searching examination of its ash, before he could bring himself to say what he had to say.

'In consequence of el Bilbanito's lamented decease,' he began, slowly, 'I must address my orders to you, señores. Those orders are —'

'Yes?' prompted Hugh O'Neill, when the pause grew too long for his patience.

'My orders are that I take the gun out of your charge. The Junta has decided that it is too valuable to risk in the plains. They have decided to employ it in the fortifications of Ferrol, whither I am to escort it at once.'

There was a shocked silence for a moment before O'Neill's anger blazed out.

'What?' he said. 'Take it all the way back again? Take it away from us? Never!'

'Those are my orders from the Junta, señores,' said the colonel, firmly. 'It is my duty to obey them. And may I remind you that it is the duty even of guerilleros to obey the established government?'

'It is simple plain foolery,' said Hugh.

'I could think of a worse name for it,' said Carlos.

'Perhaps I could too,' said the colonel, 'but I would not say it to my superior officer.'

'So they have sent no ammunition, nothing?' demanded Hugh.

'Naturally not. Why send ammunition from Ferrol when it is at Ferrol that the gun is to be used?'

'But el Bilbanito made all sorts of plans to use the gun on the plains,' said Hugh.

'I am aware of that,' said the Colonel. 'El Platero with two hundred men is waiting to meet him between here

50

and La Merced. Cesar Urquiola has brought up his cavalry. Even Mina has sent a battalion of his Navarrese to the rendezvous.'

'With a thousand men and the gun we could raid as far as the great road,' said Carlos O'Neill.

'I think it extremely likely,' said the colonel. 'You could set all Leon in an uproar. La Merced has only two hundred men in garrison, with two six-pounders.'

'Indeed?' said Hugh, professional interest quickening. 'I thought it was stronger than that. We can take it easily, then.'

'You might, if you had a gun to do it with. But unfortunately, señores, as I am the first to admit – you have no gun.'

'But you cannot take our gun from us, colonel. It would be criminal folly to waste this chance.'

The colonel had to brace himself before he could reiterate his determination. It was sad to disappoint these two young men; it was sadder still to throw away an opportunity which even the colonel's limited military instinct told him was ideal. But he had his orders, and he must abide by them.

'I must repeat, gentlemen,' he said, slowly, 'that I start for Ferrol tomorrow with the gun.'

Carlos O'Neill's chair fell over with a clatter as he got to his feet.

'We won't permit it,' he said. 'You shall *not* have our gun.'

'This sounds like insubordination,' said the colonel.

'So it is! The gun's ours and we shall keep it!'

'Don Carlos, that is not the way to speak to your superior officer. I might punish you severely if I did not make allowance for your youthful enthusiasm.'

'You will *not* have the gun. Not if I die for it.'

'Don't say words of ill omen like that, Don Carlos. Remember – gentlemen, you force me to say this – that outside I have three battalions of my regiment. Fifteen hundred men altogether. And you have – two hundred? Three hundred? If you force me to take strong measures you see that I can carry them out. And if your insubordination is maintained outside the privacy of this office I shall have to take official notice of it. I shall have to call a court-martial to try you for mutiny. There is only one penalty for mutiny, gentlemen, and you know what it is.'

For the moment the colonel thought he had won his point. Neither of the young men spoke. Carlos O'Neill even replaced his arm in the sling whence he had withdrawn it in his excitement. Then Hugh O'Neill rose from his chair, where he had been seated all through the interview. He said nothing, but walked slowly to the door; the colonel and his adjutant followed him with their eyes. So lackadaisical were his movements that no one could have suspected him of any plan. He opened the door, walked through, and shut it behind him. The colonel was genuinely sorry for him; he thought that, overwhelmed by sorrow at being deprived of his beloved gun, he had gone out to work off his despair in drink, or, possibly – for mixed Spanish and Irish blood plays queer tricks – even in exercise. The colonel was only disillusioned when he heard O'Neill's voice ringing out like a trumpet, 'Princesa! Princesa! Oh, Princesa, come and hear about this new treachery in high places!'

The men came running to hear him. They massed themselves around the gun on to which he had climbed. Irish eloquence winged his Spanish words. He told of the mountain sides over which they had dragged the gun, and of the mustering of guerilleros at the rendezvous, of the coming of el Platero and of Mina. He told them of the helpless garrisons in the plains, the prisoners who would fall into their hands, the plunder which was there for the taking, the welcome they would receive when they freed the towns from the hated French dominion. He got a roar of laughter from the plainsmen among them when he said that he was tired of the belly-aching mountain cider and wanted to drink honest wine again – it was a deft argument which appealed both to those who looked on wine as a necessity of life and those who considered it a rare luxury.

Colonel Casariego made his appearance in the mob just as O'Neill was working up to his climax, telling the men that folly or worse at headquarters had decided to waste all these glorious opportunities. The Princesa Regiment was ordered back to rot again in garrison at Ferrol, and they were to drag the gun back with them over the mountains. Carlos O'Neill sidled up to Colonel Casariego as he made his way towards an excited group of his officers. Before the colonel realized what was happening something was dug uncomfortably into his ribs and, looking down, he saw that it was the muzzle of a pistol. At O'Neill's back were half a dozen of his gang.

'I think we will go back to headquarters, colonel,' said O'Neill, politely.

The only satisfaction Colonel Casariego found as he sat miserably in his headquarters with a sentry at his door, listening to the hullabaloo outside, was in the periodical arrival of his senior officers, who came to the house under O'Neill's escort, in ones and twos, and were incontinently locked up with him. The three majors commanding battalions, the older ones among the captains, the adjutant and the quartermaster, all came to share his captivity. What was significant was the absence of the junior officers. It was no surprise at all to the colonel when Hugh O'Neill made his appearance again and announced to the waiting officers, 'Gentlemen, the Princesa Regiment has decided to follow me to the plains. Any of you officers who care to join me and serve under me, retaining your present rank, will be welcome. I only ask your word as gentlemen to give faithful service to me and the cause of Spain.'

There was only a moment's silence before Captain

Albano rose.

'I am with you, sir,' he said.

And one after the other the majors, and the captains, and the quartermaster, came over to O'Neill. Only Colonel Casariego was left, sitting solitary at the table. There was nothing left for him to do but to make his way back to the Junta and confess his failure, to tell of the desertion of his whole regiment. He bowed under his misery. His face went down into his hands, and he wept. O'Neill shut the door quietly, and left the old man weeping.

CHAPTER VIII

CAPTAIN LUKE BRETT, of His Britannic Majesty's forty-gun frigate *Parnassus*, was in his cabin reading the Bible, for he was a religious man, when a midshipman knocked on the door.

'Come in,' said Captain Brett.

'Please, sir,' said the midshipman, 'Mr Hampton says there is a fishing boat coming off from the land, apparently signalling to us.'

Captain Brett looked instinctively up at the tell-tale compass over his head.

'Tell Mr Hampton I'll be on deck directly,' he said.

He put the marker carefully between the pages of his Bible, and followed the midshipman to the quarter-deck. Last night's gale had died down by now. The *Parnassus*, close hauled under easy sail, heaved and swooped over a quartering sea, with every now and again a spatter of spray tumbling in over the starboard bow. Captain Brett's all-embracing eye swept over the ship; in that one encircling glance, as his officers well knew, he could inspect every detail of the routine of the deck. He looked at the trim of the sails, at the gleaming white decks, the shot in the racks and the hammocks in the nettings, the course of the ship, the working party overhauling cable on the forecastle. Away on the port side could be seen the brown cliffs of Spain, with Cape de las Peñas in the distance.

The first lieutenant was looking forward through his telescope, and Captain Brett, following his gaze, saw a little speck appear on the crest of a wave, disappear in a trough, and appear again, bobbing violently. It was an open fishing boat running down wind under a brown lugsail to intercept them. As the captain looked through the telescope which the lieutenant handed him he saw a speck of white run up to the top of the little mast and down again, up and down.

'Yes, they're signalling to us. Bear down two points, Mr Hampton. Heave to and let them come alongside when we reach them.'

'Shall I have a bo'sun's chair ready, sir? You know what these dagoes are.'

'As you wish, Mr Hampton.'

Lieutenant Hampton's suggestion was proved to be a very sensible one, for the man who was swung eventually on to the *Parnassus'* deck from the yard-arm clearly could not have climbed a rope. He had one arm in a sling, but that was not the most important of his disabilities. He was green with sea-sickness as a result of the violent motion of the fishing boat; moreover, to Mr Hampton's huge disgust, his feet were no sooner on the deck than he vomited again, helplessly, holding on with his one hand to the rope of the bo'sun's chair over his head.

'God damn all dagoes,' said Mr Hampton.

When the paroxysm passed the man looked about him. He was a tall, slender man, dressed in something resembling uniform – a much patched blue coat with some gold lace still adherent, and white breeches and boots and spurs; perhaps it was the first time that spurs had ever jingled on the deck of the *Parnassus*.

'El capitan?' he asked, inquiringly.

'I am Captain Brett, of this ship.'

Clearly the man spoke no English; the words meant nothing to him, but at sight of Captain Brett's uniform, shabby though it was, and air of authority, he decided that Captain Brett was the man he sought. He produced from his pocket a small leather wallet, and with infinite care he drew a letter from it and offered it to the captain. It was an innocent-looking enough letter, although it would have been his death warrant if he had fallen into the hands of the French with it on his person. The captain glanced through it, examined the signature with care, and passed it on to his lieutenant, who read:

OFFICE OF H.M.'S MISSION TO THE ASTURIAS

GIJON

10th June 1810

This is to make known to officers of His Britannic Majesty's forces by land or sea that the bearer of this recommendation, Captain Carlos O'Neill of the Spanish Artillery, is an officer in the Partisan forces of Spain, and to charge all such officers to render all assistance to Captain O'Neill as their duty permits and as they may judge will further the common cause.

HENRY BERKELY, Major

H.M.'s representative in the Asturias

Second Foot Guards

'That's Berkely's signature all right,' said Captain Brett, 'I've seen one of these things before. And what's this he's trying to show us now?'

Captain O'Neill was trying to draw another paper from his wallet, which fitted it so tightly that in his one-handed condition he found difficulty in drawing it out.

'Allow me, captain,' said Captain Brett; the fellow's bowings and scrapings had actually infected him, too.

Captain Brett drew out the paper; it had been long folded and was in danger of tearing along the creases.

'Oh, it's his commission,' said Captain Brett.

It was indeed a noble document, embossed at the head with the arms of Spain and bearing three seals at the foot; it was printed in type resembling a flowing italic hand, but quite incomprehensible to Captain Brett because it was in the Spanish language. But he could see that written in by hand here and there through the document in gaps purposely left were the words 'Don Carlos O'Neill'. It was obviously a genuine document, and established the identity of the bearer.

'If his name's O'Neill, why the devil doesn't he speak English?' asked Lieutenant Hampton.

'He's a Spanish-Irishman. I've seen his sort before,' said Captain Brett. 'He had better have a drink while we find out what he wants.'

The gesture of offering a drink is an easy one, actually within the capacity of a stiff-necked naval captain; while he made it Captain Brett heard a chuckle from the midshipman of the watch at his side, but Lieutenant Hampton, that resolute disciplinarian, saved his captain's dignity.

'Fore to'gan masthead, Mr Norman,' he said. 'And stay there until sunset.'

And the midshipman went, crestfallen, while Captain Brett escorted Captain O'Neill with ceremony to the companion ladder. But once down below, where everything heaved and creaked and swayed, O'Neill's misgivings overpowered him. Unceremoniously he turned and rushed up the ladder again and fell limply across the leeside bulwarks.

'Poor fellow,' said Captain Brett. 'A glass of my old port ought to do him good.'

The captain's steward brought chairs and bottles and glasses, and, once seated, with a glass of brandied port inside him (where, for a miracle, it stayed), O'Neill seemed to get better.

'Now, captain, tell me what I can do for you,' said Captain Brett.

The words meant nothing to the Spaniard, but the tone in which they were spoken did. He got out of his chair, and looked round the ship. The twelve-pounders down on the main deck clearly, from his attitude, were not what he sought. But he went across to the big eighteen-pounder quarterdeck carronade, looked at it with delight, took out the tompion, examined the bore, and then slapped the gun with pleasure, pointed to himself, and then at the distant shore.

'He wants to take our eighteen-pounder away with him!' said Lieutenant Hampton.

'I don't often swear,' said Captain Brett, 'but I'll see him damned before he does.'

Both officers shook their heads violently, and O'Neill's face fell until he realized that they misunderstood him.

'What's he looking for now?' asked the lieutenant.

'He's found it,' said the captain.

O'Neill, after staring anxiously round, had seen hanging by the wheel the slate and pencil of the log of the watch. He rushed and seized these, and began hurriedly drawing with the slate on his knee. After three minutes he showed them the results of his work – a neat drawing of a big gun on a military carriage. He pointed to the picture, and then he moved his hand in a circle round the muzzle of the carronade, and then out to the mountains again, and then to his chest.

'He's got an eighteen-pounder on shore,' said Captain Brett, and nodded and smiled, trying not to look quite as foolish as he felt.

Thus encouraged, O'Neill started drawing again.

'What in God's name is this?' asked Hampton, who was looking at the drawing upside down as it progressed. 'Grapes?'

'No, shot, of course,' said Captain Brett. It was a picture of a pyramid of cannon balls.

Brett opened the shot rack beside the carronade, and lifted out one of the eighteen-pounder shot and offered it inquiringly to O'Neill.

'Si, si, si,' said the latter, nodding ecstatically.

'At last!' said Brett.

But O'Neill was drawing again, excitedly.

Now that they were on the track only a cursory glance was necessary to recognize the new drawing as a picture of a powder barrel.

'He wants powder and shot for an eighteen-pounder siege gun on shore,' decided Captain Brett. 'He can have them.'

One paragraph of his orders laid stress on the need to help the Spanish forces, and to co-operate with them wherever possible. It was only English sea power, reaching out across hundreds of miles of ocean, which sustained the Spaniards in their interminable struggle with the French Empire. But for that, the Spanish insurrection would long before have been quenched in blood as had been the Tyrolese revolt, and the Lombard revolt in preceding years.

'I don't know how he thinks he'll get them, sir,' said Hampton inquiringly. 'The French have got every port garrisoned between here and Ferrol.'

'He knows some quiet inlet or other, never fear,' replied Brett. 'Look, he's drawing again.'

The new picture was unmistakably a mule – not a donkey or a horse, because O'Neill's pencil point laid great stress on the ears and tail. Then O'Neill spread the fingers of his one sound hand ten times, and pointed down the coast.

'He's got fifty mules waiting somewhere,' said Hampton.

It was Captain Brett who solved the difficulty of finding out the exact place; O'Neill could think of no method of conveying his meaning, for all his pointing and gesticulating.

'The chart, Mr Hampton,' said Captain Brett.

With the chart of the coast spread out before him O'Neill had no difficulty in pointing out the exact little bay he had in mind. Everybody this time was nodding and smiling, pleased with the progress made despite all difficulties.

'He's drawing again,' said Hampton.

O'Neill was making an addition to his picture of the mule; when he passed it over it had along its side five cannon balls held in a sack over its back.

'That means ten altogether to each mule,' commented Brett. 'They always overload the poor brutes.'

Next the cannon balls were rubbed out by O'Neill's wetted finger and replaced by a powder barrel. O'Neill pointed at the mule so adorned and then spread his fingers.

'He means he wants five loads of powder, and forty-five of shot – four hundred and fifty rounds. Let me see.' Captain Brett was not of a really agile mental quality, but he succeeded in solving the problem of mental arithmetic presented to him.

'Yes, he's about right. That is not quite enough powder, but I suppose it is easier for them to get powder than eighteen-pounder shot.'

'That's four tons of shot, besides the powder, sir,' said Hampton, who also had been doing mental arithmetic. 'It'll mean sending the cutter – that boat of his isn't nearly big enough.'

'That is so,' said Brett.

The two officers looked at each other, and then found themselves glancing uneasily at O'Neill as if he could read their thoughts although not understanding their speech.

'It might be a trap, sir.'

'Very true, Mr Hampton. You will have to use all precautions. Have the four-pounder mounted in the cutter, and loaded with grape. Get that boat of his in tow, and I will stand in after dark. You can cast off *here*' – Brett's stubby finger indicated the mouth of the inlet – 'and I will wait for you.'

'Yes, sir.'

'And call the gunner and see to breaking out the shot and powder he wants. Offer him a few rounds of canister and grape as well as round shot. He may need 'em, sometime.'

'Aye, aye, sir.'

'If it *is* a trap, Mr Hampton, that boat will be just ahead of the cutter as you go in. Fire the gun into it, and then come back, bringing this gentleman with you. We will see how he looks at the yard-arm.'

'Aye, aye, sir.'

There is no need to follow Captain Brett and Mr Hampton through the complicated task of explaining to Carlos O'Neill in dumb show the fact that he was their prisoner until the cutter should leave the inlet after nightfall unharmed. The rising moon found the *Parnassus*, a shimmering white ghost of a ship, hove to off the mouth of the bay. Captain Brett, leaning on the quarter-deck rail, had felt so much confidence in O'Neill's obvious honesty that he was not in the least surprised or relieved when he heard the splash of oars returning down the bay and knew that the munitions had been safely landed. Mr Hampton came on board to make his report.

'Yes, Mr Hampton?'

'Everything was as he said, sir. The mules were waiting on the beach. I saw them loaded and start up a little path up the cliff.'

'Very good, Mr Hampton, hoist the cutter in.'

But it was a different story five days afterwards when Captain Brett came on board again after going on shore for orders at Ferrol.

'Oh, Mr Hampton,' he said, 'do you remember that man O'Neill who came on board when we were off Cape de las Peñas? If ever we see him again we are to put him in irons and bring him here for trial.'

'For trial, sir?'

'Yes, they want him for treason, and mutiny, and – bless my soul, there's no end to his crimes. Berkely gobbled like a turkey at the mention of his name?'

'Was that recommendation of his a forgery, then, sir?'

'No, but it was a year old. We noticed that. And since Berkely gave it to him – just before he came off to us, in fact – he has got half the Spanish army to mutiny and taken them off on the opposite course to what Berkely ordered. The Junta is sick with rage about it.'

'But what did he want the ammunition for, sir?'

'For his eighteen-pounder. It's the only siege gun in all Galicia, it appears. The Junta wanted it for themselves, it appears, and O'Neill thought otherwise.'

'He seemed to me to be a man of sound judgment, sir.'

But Captain Brett did not try to countenance any criticism, however veiled, of the government of His Majesty's Peninsular allies.

CHAPTER IX

WHILE Hugh O'Neill was waiting for his brother's return he came to know all the sensations of a man in a powder magazine with the building on fire. The idiocy of the Junta in not sending the ammunition which el Bilbanito had demanded was imposing delays on the invasion of Leon, and delays were dangerous. There was no fear of the French; with Wellington loose again in the South and every French resource at strain to hold him in check the French were content to sit quiet in their garrisons in the North and hope not to be attacked. Every movable body of troops in Leon was on the march for the Tagus, as O'Neill well knew, and he had little to fear that any news of the concentration in the mountains would leak out to them. Nor was there much to fear at the moment from the Junta. That was two hundred miles away, at Ferrol, and it would be long before the news of the defection of the Princesa Regiment reached it; it would be longer still before they could move up troops – if they had any to spare – to interfere with him.

The danger lay round about him, close upon him. Troops which had mutinied once might mutiny again. He had seduced them from their allegiance by a promise of an invasion of Leon; with every day that the invasion was postponed their turbulence increased. The fact that there was no ammunition for the gun would be attributed to his negligence, and no mob ever stops to listen to excuses. O'Neill, a year or two ago while he was still with the army, had seen San Juan, a real general, hung up in a tree by his mutinous troops and then used as a target. Something like that would be his fate if he had to hold these undisciplined villains in check much longer.

It was a blessing that Carlos had been able to move off at once in search of ammunition. The Princesa Regiment's mule train had been at his disposition, and fortunately Carlos still had the recommendation to the English which Colonel Berkely had given him nearly a year before. The sea was only thirty miles away, across three ranges of mountains. Hugh O'Neill tried to be pessimistic in his estimate of the time Carlos would be gone. He decided that Carlos might be back in a week, and he set himself to keep things quiet for that time. He called out the Princesa Regiment for manoeuvres and worked them until they were ready to drop. He sent the guerilleros, both those of his own band and those of the deceased el Bilbanito, on expeditions hither and thither to harry the wretched villages for food – he had nearly two thousand men to feed, and the whole district had been plundered and replundered for years. He sent urgent messages to el Platero – the silversmith – and to Joaquin Alvarez, Mina's lieutenant, and to Don Cesar Urquiola, begging them to have patience and await his arrival at the rendezvous. But all the same it was a mighty relief to the young man when a boy rode up on a pony with a note from Carlos. He was on his way back with the ammunition, and would reach them shortly. O'Neill called down a blessing on the British Navy and issued the order to his motley forces to make ready to get on the move. The animals were harnessed up to the gun and they set out on the last stage of the journey through the mountains.

The gun, the big lumbering thing, was responsible for much already. Here, on the edge of the mountains, was assembled the biggest concentration of irregular troops the war had yet seen. Besides the Princesa Regiment there was O'Neill's band and el Bilbanito's. There was Alvarez with his Navarrese, whom Mina had sent from their Pyrenean hunting grounds. There was el Platero with his Biscayans, and Urquiola with his Castilian horsemen – the only guerilla troops who had dared to carry on the war in the plains. They were of a different type from the mountaineers, lean, dignified men, who wore their clothes and their beards with an air. Pennons fluttered at their lance points when they trotted up to meet the descending column, and their spurs and accoutrements jingled bravely. Yet Urquiola and el Platero and Joaquin Alvarez all greeted O'Neill with deference when they came up to him as he rode beside the gun. It was not the two thousand men whom he commanded who made them so respectful; it was the gun. Its thirteen feet of length, its five-foot wheels, its immense breech, all indicated its colossal power.

One and all, those men had chafed at the restraint imposed upon them by the little fortress in the plains. This gun would knock those places to pieces.

On the evening when the forces were all met, O'Neill and his brother walked out to where the mountains definitely ceased, along a path which ran along the top of a huge green spur jutting from the mountains into the plain. Here, were the hill fell away in a steep escarpment, they could look out over the plain, and note the winding rivers and the scattered villages, and the rich fields and the numerous roads. It was from this very point that el Bilbanito had stood gazing out over the plain, a long time ago, and wishing that he had artillery with which to descend into it, but neither of the young men were aware of that, and perhaps if they had been they would not have considered it a matter of ill omen. Their hearts were high, and they laughed as they laid their plans. Carlos O'Neill even considered it now worth that loss of dignity which he had suffered on his visit to HMS *Parnassus*, worth the sea-sickness and the childish drawing on the slate and the gesticulations which had (in his opinion) consorted ill with the gravity of a Spanish gentleman with the blood of kings in his veins.

CHAPTER X

MAJOR JONQUIER was a Dutchman He was a fat, pale, fair man with pale blue eyes, slightly protruding. He was not much given to thought; he never meditated upon the strangeness of the fate which made Holland a part of France, and which had carried him off from his land of dykes and windmills, and had set him down in command of a mass of French conscripts in the sun-soaked plains of Spain, and had bestowed upon him the high-sounding title of Governor of La Merced, and had set him to hold Spaniards in subjection to a Corsican who was known as Emperor of the French.

He was a man of phlegmatic temperament, but he was a little annoyed when a message came to him, just when he was comfortably dining, to the effect that there were enemies in sight. With a sigh he got up from the table, and rebuttoned his tunic, and refastened his stock, and buckled his sword-belt round his bulging waist, and drained his glass of wine, and took his telescope from its hooks on the wall, and then, sighing again, he addressed himself to the climb up the steep stone stairs to the first floor, and he positively grunted with the exertion of climbing the vertical ladder which led to the roof. If the sentry had allowed his imagination to run away with him, he would get a week's *salle de police* for disturbing him at this, the most sacred hour of the day.

Determined to get the business over and done with without delay, he did not linger on the roof, but walked straightway over to the bell tower, bowed his head to enter by the low door, and climbed ponderously up the little ladder to the little square platform at the summit, where the French flag flapped languidly in the slight wind. The sentry was there, and the sergeant of the guard, and the addition of Major Jonquier's portly form made the platform uncomfortably crowded when he squeezed through the trapdoor.

He extended his telescope and looked about him, and the sergeant of the guard pointed excitedly towards where the mountains towered up from the plain.

'Hum!' said the major to himself, and again, 'Hum!'

There was something which looked like a snake a mile long advancing up the road from the mountains, where the sun was about to set in scarlet glory. From the length it must be a small army, but it was so wreathed in dust that nothing could be definitely ascertained, except that through the dust occasionally could be seen the flash of weapons. But ahead of the column the governor could plainly see more of the enemy. There was a small column of horsemen on the road, and out to right and to the left of it were smaller groups of cavalry winding their way along the field-paths parallel to the road. Clearly

66

there was a strong force of the enemy advancing to the attack of the fort, screened, as the best military operation dictated, by an advance guard of cavalry. As the major's glass swept the plain again his eye caught sight of something fluttering where the cavalry rode. They were lance pennons – it must be Urquiola and his mounted brigands come up from Castile. Once before they had penetrated this far. There must be a concentration of guerilleros – an event often expected but never witnessed before.

Major Jonquier began issuing his orders even before he left the platform. The messenger was to ride at once to Leon with news of the attack. Major Jonquier was quite certain that the messenger would not do any good; he knew that in all the province there was no relieving force which could be sent to him at present. The monthly convoy of supplies with its heavy escort was only due to arrive in three weeks' time. But the garrison – an unreliable lot – would be more cheerful if they knew the messenger had ridden off.

Meanwhile for three weeks the major was equally certain that he could hold off the attack of any mob of irregulars, who of course would be without artillery. He came down into the fort and began a rapid inspection of the defences.

La Merced had been a convent, a large square building of grey stone built round a central courtyard. Its position for the defence of the bridge was ideal. It stood on a rounded hillock just away from the river and a complete hundred yards from the roadway where it joined the bridge. At one time the land on which it stood had been enclosed by a high stone wall, but this had been torn down because of the protection it might offer an attacking force, and had been replaced by a high strong palisade of wood, of which the posts stood just far enough apart to prevent a man squeezing through. This palisade would delay any storming party, and as it stood within comfortable musket range of the convent it formed an important part of the defences. The building itself, like many Spanish convents, offered windows only towards the courtyard; the four exterior walls were quite blank, save for the loopholes which the garrison had knocked in them all round. The stone which had once formed the park wall had all been carted up to the convent and built into two little bastions at opposite corners, in each of which was mounted a six-pounder, one commanding the bridge and the other the road. Each gun could fire along two faces of the building, so that if the attackers were even able to climb the palisade they would find themselves merely at the foot of the blank walls, pelted with musketry from the loopholes and scoured with an enfilading fire of grape from the guns. No wonder Major Jonquier felt easy in his mind as he went along the corridors seeing that everything was in order.

One of his two companies of infantry was on duty, the men standing at the loopholes looking out; the other company, instead of making the most of its period off duty, like sensible men, were gathered about in groups in the barrack rooms, or peeping out of the loopholes, discussing the new development. But then, they were only recruits, not veteran troops.

Major Jonquier went out on to each bastion in turn. At each gun were five artillerymen. The linstocks were burning and the guns were loaded ready with grape. With a grunt of satisfaction he waddled back again into the convent. He peeped into the courtyard. His six cows were there, in improvised wooden stalls – Major Jonquier was a man who insisted on milk in his coffee and butter on his bread. He saw that the sentries keeping guard over the doors of the cellars in which were the stores were at their posts. He gave orders for carcasses – bundles of rags soaked in oil – to be made ready on the parapets. If these were to be lighted and tossed over they would give all the light necessary to shoot down the attackers in the event of a night attack. Night was already falling rapidly, and it would be dark before the raiding army reached the convent.

He went back into his own room and shouted to his servant for his dinner. That servant was a perfect fool. He had the incredible imbecility to bring in to the major the omelet which had been ready to serve before the alarm – it was a nightmare of an omelet now; as the major said, with oaths, it was the colour, shape, consistency, and toughness of the sole of a shoe. He drove the man out to the kitchen to prepare another.

It was no excuse for the man that he was a Spaniard and would be hanged for certain if the place were taken. The place was not going to be taken, and an omelet was a more important matter than a Spaniard's neck, anyway. The second omelet was only a slight improvement. Major Jonquier groaned as he ate it; the man's nerve must have been completely ruined by his fright. But the braised beef with red pepper would be better – Major Jonquier had prepared that dish with his own painstaking hands before this bother about guerilleros had begun. He ate it hungrily, heard with annoyance that there was no soft cheese to complete the meal, and contented himself with hard. He finished his wine, and shouted for his coffee and brandy. He stretched his legs beneath the oak table and tried to feel like a man who has dined satisfactorily. It was a useless effort. A dinner interrupted halfway through can never be a good dinner. The bleak grey stone room was too Spartan by far for his tastes, and it was so infernally cold, despite its miserable brazero of charcoal, that he had to wrap his cloak round his legs. The tallow dips gave only a suspicion of light. The coffee was not coffee at all, but only a horrible chicory substitute which the continental blockade forced him to drink. His cigar was perfectly foul. Major Jonquier thought of his native Holland, of white-tiled stoves and oil lamps and good coffee and a black cigar with a straw up the middle. The only thing which was satisfactory was the brandy, and even of that he did not think it advisable to drink more than three glasses after his couple of litres of wine. The horrors of war were decidedly unpleasant.

He could not even drink his brandy in peace because that young fool Captain Dupont insisted on coming in to tell him that the guerilleros were in earshot. The major growled like a bear, climbed up to the roof again, and peered through the night over the parapet. Decidedly there was activity out there in the darkness. The major and the captain could hear voices, shouting, and laughter. The neighing of a horse came distinctly up to them. Then a new sound reached their ears – the chink of spades and pickaxes. Some working party out there was digging vigorously. Major Jonquier decided it must be on the summit of the mound lower down the road, a quarter of a mile away. What they could be digging was more than he could guess – barricades, probably, across the road as a defence against cavalry. He knew by experience that those guerilleros from the mountains, who had half of them been miners in the days of honest work, would dig like badgers on the slightest provocation, huge, useless fortifications, always in the wrong place.

He was tempted to go down to the bastion and order a shot or two in that direction, but he decided against it; ranging and aiming were too difficult in the dark. He impressed upon Dupont the need to keep the sentries well awake, so that they would hear if anyone tried to chop down a section of the palisade under cover of the darkness. He himself repeated his tour of inspection, and testily ordered the young men of the company off duty to get to bed and go to sleep. The whole garrison would have to be on duty an hour before dawn. Major Jonquier confidently expected that the guerilleros would try their usual tactics – a wild rush in the grey of the early morning.

They could do so if they liked. He could predict the result, having fought guerilleros often enough before. Many men would die at the palisades. A few ardent spirits would perhaps hew a little gap. A few others would haul heavy scaling ladders up the slope, but they would not even reach the foot of the wall. They would be shot as they climbed under their burdens, and finally the whole mob would break up and run and probably not stop until they reached the mountains again. It would be a salutary lesson for them, and for another few weeks he would be able to dine undisturbed and sleep in peace. As it was he went and lay down on his bed with all his clothes on, even his sword as well, leaving strict orders that he should be called before daylight.

In the dark morning when his servant came to wake him he started out of bed as soon as he was called. Pulling his cloak close round him in the biting cold he walked out into the dark corridors. The passages rang with the sound of the heavy boots of the men coming up to take their posts at the loopholes. All of them were shuddering with cold. Jonquier turned to the sergeant at his side.

'Have the soup heated and brought to the men at their posts,' he ordered.

He went up on to the flat roof where Dupont was nervously pacing about. The young fool had evidently not been to bed, and the major was about to reprimand him severely when his words were cut short by a new series of sounds down by the road. There was a cracking of whips and a clanking of chains. Lights showed, flickering, over by the mound.

'What in hell —?' said Jonquier, peering vainly through the darkness. The lights moved vaguely about. Someone shouted hoarsely. There was a terrific bustle over there.

'Oh, well, we shall know soon enough,' said Jonquier, philosophically.

The eastern horizon was just beginning to grow a little

paler, and it became evident that it was going to be a misty morning.

'Keep your men awake up here, Dupont,' said Major Jonquier. 'And remember never to leave any side of the fort unguarded, however hard they may be attacking the other ones.'

He lowered himself down the ladder and reached the first floor. The men were all at their posts here, and as he descended a private came clattering along with a pail of soup, and another followed behind with a basket of bread.

'If they attack,' he said to the nearest group, 'don't get muddled. Don't drink your muskets and fire your soup out of the loopholes.'

The men laughed. Everyone liked old pot-bellied Jonquier and his funny guttural French.

'And aim low,' said Jonquier more seriously. 'Aim for their legs and put an end to their fandangoes.'

He waddled down the staircase to the ground floor. Everyone down here had finished their breakfast.

'Feeling better for your breakfast, men?' he asked. 'That's good. Now you won't —' He made the same joke as he had made on the first floor, and got the same laugh.

'And aim low,' he went on just as before. 'Aim —'

Jonquier was doing his duty. He was cheering up his soldiers, and embedding the pill of good advice in the jam of banter.

He went to a loophole and peered out. By now it was nearly full light, and the mist was beginning to shred away. If the guerilleros were going to attack, they were losing their best opportunity. The big bulk of the fort must be fully visible to them by now. It was strange that they should delay. He walked through into the big grey stone room which had been the refectory and which ran along the whole of one side of the building, facing towards the mound down by the road.

'Feeling better for your breakfast, men?' he asked. 'That's —'

A terrific crash interrupted him. The building shook, and the whole hall was filled with stone dust and flying chips of stone. Someone screamed. Something fell on the stone floor with a clang and rolled towards Jonquier. It was a big cannon ball – a most certain indication that La Merced was doomed. Jonquier looked at it as though death itself was rolling towards him over the floor – as indeed it was. A big section of the two-foot thick wall had been knocked in, leaving a nearly circular hole two feet in diameter between two loopholes. The unhewn stones of which the wall was composed had been sent flying to all parts of the room. A man with a shattered wrist was still screaming, as much with fright as with pain.

'Stop that noise!' said Jonquier, pulling himself together. 'Go down into the store-room and get one of the servants to bandage that arm for you. Get to your posts, men.'

With all the appearance of nonchalance that he could assume he walked to the hole the cannon ball had made and looked through it. There was still a slight mist outside, but it would hardly last five minutes longer with the thirsty sun drinking it up. Down there by the mound the mist seemed thicker. No, it was a cloud of powder smoke which was gradually dissipating. Jonquier could make out the raw brown of the newly turned earth; five seconds later the smoke had drifted sufficiently away for him to see, vaguely, a rude breastwork which had been dug. And pointing out through the embrasure of the earthwork he could see the muzzle of a big gun. Even as he looked the gun disappeared in a burst of white smoke, and in the same instant the building shook again to a splintering crash as the shot hit the wall twenty feet from where he was standing. The concussion threw him to the floor.

There was panic in the long hall, but Jonquier dragged

himself to his feet in time check it.

'Back to your posts, you cowards!' he roared. 'You, sergeant, shoot the next man to flinch.'

The men hesitated, but Jonquier stood firm.

'Each man must lie down by his loophole,' he said. 'And stand up and aim straight when the rush comes. I am going to turn the guns on their battery. We'll not be hit without hitting back.'

On the first floor he saw young Lieutenant Lecamus fidgeting with his sword hilt and biting his lips with nervousness. Even as they met the building shook again as another shot hit the wall below.

'Go down to the refectory and keep the men there up to the mark,' Jonquier ordered. 'And pull yourself together first, man.'

He brushed the grey dust from his salient abdomen, and, wheezing a little, hurried on to the bastion. Here the gunners were standing to their gun.

'Why the devil haven't you opened fire?' he demanded.

'No orders, sir,' said the sergeant in charge.

'Orders? Who waits for orders in a siege? You're not fit for your job, sergeant. Slew the gun round and open fire with round shot on that breastwork. No, don't stop to draw that charge. Fire the grape out.'

The gun roared out its defiance, but it was a much more insignificant sound than the deep-mouthed bellow of the big siege gun which the guerilleros had somehow acquired. In the smoke the artillerymen sponged out the gun, rammed in cartridge and ball, and the sergeant crouched over the breech to aim. He stepped aside and jerked the lanyard. Jonquier saw the earth fly from the wing of the breastwork.

'High and to the right,' he said. 'Reload.'

Then the big gun on the mound fired back, and this time the shot hit the solid mass of the bastion six feet below their feet.

'Ha!' said Jonquier. 'We've taught them to leave the wall alone.'

The sergeant fired the gun again, but this time it was a clean miss. No one saw where the shot fell.

'Reload,' said Jonquier. 'I will lay the gun next time.'

As he spoke the big gun on the mound thundered forth its reply, and the ball screamed through the air close over their heads.

'Devilish good gunners down there,' said Jonquier to himself. 'And a devilish good gun.'

He crouched over the breech, looking through the notch on the elevator bar and the groove on the muzzle swell. In the bit of the interior of the breastwork which he could see through the embrasure he saw bare-armed figures labouring over the siege gun. He aimed carefully, and signed to the sergeant to fire while he moved aside to note the effect. This time earth flew from the face of the earthwork close to the embrasure.

'We'll hit him next round,' said Jonquier. The gun was wiped out, the cartridge rammed, and a gunner was about to thrust the ball into the muzzle when the reply came. Eighteen pounds of solid iron, flying at three hundred yards a second, hit the little six-pounder square on the mouth. The air was full of flying bits, and the gun was flung back off its carriage. It was split clean open for half its length, one trunnion broken off, the carriage knocked to pieces. The gunner with the cannon ball fell dead with a fragment of iron through his neck.

Jonquier looked down at the wreck and ruin. He was of the type that failure merely makes angry, not despairing. The blood surged into his face. He clenched his hands and stamped his feet. But by an effort of will he prevented himself from shaking his impotent fists at the enemy and compelled himself to speak calmly and carelessly.

'Our gun receives an honourabe discharge,' he said. 'Get your muskets and lie down, you men. Save your fire when the rush comes until they are at the foot of the wall.'

He climbed back out of the bastion on to the roof again, and walked over to the other bastion. As he went he felt the fort tremble again as another shot hit the wall below. The Spaniards had recommenced, pitilessly, pounding at the main building to open a breach.

The reason why the other gun had not opened fire was obvious. The angle of the fort projected between it and the siege battery. There was nothing to fire at. Jonquier played with the idea of hoisting the gun up to the roof, running it across, and lowering it down to take the place of the injured gun, but he abandoned it. Even a six-pounder is a difficult and ponderous thing to hoist about, and the breach might be achieved and the assault made while the gun was still out of action. Besides, this gun had been mounted to sweep the bridge; the whole reason of La Merced's existence was to guard the bridge. Removing the gun from the bastion would leave to the Spaniards practically free passage over the river.

He looked down towards the bridge and the river and caught his breath. The enemy were already over the river. He could see little knots and groups of men on the farther bank. Presumably they had crossed lower down during the night by small boats. Now a little group of men ran on to the bridge. Some of them waved their arms. Jonquier wished he had his telescope with him so that he could make out details, but he was only three hundred yards from the bridge and could see well enough. One member of the group seemed to be walking unwillingly, as if he were being dragged along. Another leaned over the parapet of the bridge as if he were fastening something to it. Then, with a bustle and a scurry the unwilling man was hoisted up and flung over the parapet. Jonquier heard the artillerymen standing beside him breathing suddenly hard. The unwilling man's fall from the parapet was abruptly checked. It ended with a jerk, which threw his arms and legs into the air in grotesque attitudes like a child's toy. Then he swung idly like a pendulum in a little arc, turning first his back to the fort and then his face, and his bald head shone in the newly risen sun. Then Jonquier recognized him; it was Julio Coppola, the renegade Spanish postboy, whom he had sent out the night before with the news of the attack. Jonquier shrugged his shoulders. Even if he had got through, it was much to be doubted if help could have come for another fortnight; but all the same, it was annoying that the Spaniards should have hanged him so publicly, because otherwise he might have told his men that help might come any moment, and so stimulated them to beat off the attack.

'Don't hang about gaping like this,' he snarled to the artillerymen. 'Sweep that rabble off the bridge.'

The men seemed to wake from an evil dream, and sprang guiltily to the gun; the whole hanging had only taken a few seconds. While they were aiming the Spaniards were scuttling back across the river like naughty boys discovered in mischief. It was almost too late when at last the gun was fired. The grape shot plunged down to the roadway of the bridge, ploughing it up, and sending chips flying from the parapets. Only one shot found its target. One of the men, hit in the leg, was thrown to the ground, and, prostrate, continued to writhe comically towards safety. The others were all safely hidden in the undergrowth along the river bank.

'Reload,' growled Jonquier, 'and keep that bridge clear in future.'

He went back over the roof and down to the refectory. The room here was thick with dust, but enough light came in through the gaping holes in the wall to show the damage which had been done. There were big ragged rents everywhere along it; the floor was littered with the stones which had been flung in. As Jonquier stood gazing round another cannon ball arrived, sent flying a big stone which was projecting into one of the holes, passed across the room, knocking a table into splinters, and crashed through the inner wall into the kitchen beyond. The men were crouching as close to the floor as they could, lying still like dead men, all save Lieutenant Lecamus, who was walking up and down trying to be brave.

'Can't I take the men out of here?' said Lecamus, as plaintively as he could whisper. 'They would be safe enough in the cellars, and we could call them out when the attack comes.'

'If we once let them down into the cellars,' replied Jonquier, 'there will be no getting them out again when the attack comes. You know that as well as I do. It will do them good to be shot over a little.' He did not add 'and you, too', although he thought it.

The pitiless pounding went on. Monotonously, every few minutes, a fresh hole appeared in the wall. The Spaniards were breaking it from end to end, and a good gun they must have had, and reliable powder, because there was very little variation in the height up the wall at which the balls hit – three feet or so. Then with a rumble and a crash a whole section of the wall, completely cut away at the bottom, came tumbling down, cascading partly into the room. Jonquier sprang forward. He was sure that the sight of that wall falling would draw the Spaniards to make their assault. One good attack, beaten back with heavy loss, would take the heart out of them and stiffen up his men. But the attack did not come. Looking out from the breach Jonquier saw no enemies. The gentle wind had blown a long smear of smoke across the country from the enemy's battery, and that was all. The dazzling sunshine revealed no column of attack. The enemy were all hidden away out of sight, behind the mound, and under the embankment of the road.

'How much ammunition have the bastards got?' asked Jonquier of himself. 'Are they going to pound the whole place into ruins before they attack?'

The only answer to the question was another shot, which hit the wall towards one end and brought down yet another big section of the crumbling structure, and another shot after that, and another, remorselessly.

Then at last came a break. Jonquier heard the high notes of a cavalry trumpet twice repeated. Two men appeared over the earthwork on the mound, and began to walk steadily towards the fort, first down the slope, and then up the gentle incline to the palisades. One had a bit of white cloth on a stick; the other blew his call upon his trumpet.

'All the etiquette of war!' sneered Jonquier to himself. 'A flag of truce and a trumpet like one gentleman to another.'

He was about to step through the breach to meet them, but checked himself. There was no need to make too much disclosure of the practicability of the gap. He turned back through the kitchen and the hall, and went out through the main door, and round the building to where the trumpeter and the flag of truce were standing at the palisades.

The trumpeter was a Basque to judge by his round blue cap – some Pyrenean smuggler, doubtless. The other wore some fragments of the blue uniform of one of the mercenary regiments of the Bourbon kings of Spain. Jonquier stopped five yards from them and stood waiting for them to speak. The officer turned to the trumpeter and said something to him, and in turn the trumpeter addressed Jonquier, speaking the vilest French.

'You must surrender,' said he.

'I shall not surrender,' said Jonquier.

The trumpeter and the officer conferred, and then the trumpeter turned to Jonquier again.

'If you surrender,' he said, 'we shall grant you your lives. If you do not, you will all be killed. That is what the laws

79

of war say.'

'I do not discuss the laws of war with brigands,' said Jonquier. 'I am an officer of the Emperor. And I trust that when General Kellermann's dragoons arrive this afternoon I shall have the pleasure of seeing you on the end of a rope.'

That was the best he could think of in the way of stimulating the besiegers to make a premature assault. He turned his back and walked away, striving to be as dignified as possible in the eyes of his men, whom he knew would be watching this interview from the parapets and loopholes. He trailed his sword and he stuck out his chest and cocked his shako.

'This is your last chance,' called the trumpeter harshly through the palisades after him.

Jonquier made no sign of having heard, and left them to turn away with no appearance of dignity. Even trifles like that may affect the spirits of troops.

It is hard to say what motive made Jonquier so obstinate in the face of death. He cannot have had overwhelming confidence in his troops to beat off an attack. He had no hope of relief. He was fighting in a cause in which he did not feel any interest. Possibly it was sheer blind obstinacy, the obstinacy of a man who finds a piece of work to his hand and will not abandon it though it kills him. Perhaps it was fighting madness, or its latter-day equivalent, professional pride. But it was hard to associate either of these qualities with the fat little man – whose blue tunic rode up in horizontal creases over his belly – despite the military splendour of his red epaulets and glittering buttons.

Lieutenant Lecamus awaited him anxiously in the refectory, and the men stood about wishful to hear what he had to say.

'You had better lie down, men,' was what he vouchsafed, 'they will be opening fire again soon.'

And then, when they had obeyed, disappointed, he continued:

'You'll soon get your revenge for being shot at. Each of you can kill six of them, while they come up the slope. But one or two each will be enough to set them running back again.'

His words were emphasized by the bellowing roar once more of the siege gun on the mound. But no shot hit the fort.

Curious that they should have missed, thought Jonquier. There came another roar from the gun, and still no sound of the impact of the ball. He went up to the roof where Captain Dupont still stood with his company crouched behind the parapet. From the roof he could see the explanation. The enemy were firing grape at the palisades. They were making good practice, too. Jonquier saw a blast of grape hit the ground six feet before the palisades, tear it up, and then, continuing on, cut off short a full dozen of the stout posts. Five rounds of grape cut enough gaps in the palisade for fifty men to make their way through at once.

Still Jonquier did not care. From the parapet of the roof, from the bastion, and from the breach itself he could turn a hundred muskets upon the attackers when they came up over the glacis. If his men held their weapons straight the enemy could not break in. Struck with a new thought he sent Captain Dupont's drummer flying down to the servants huddled in the cellars – renegade Spaniards, all of them. They were to bring up to the roof all the spare muskets and ammunition. All the men there could have two muskets each, and the servants could help with the reloading.

Until this reinforcement arrived Jonquier was in a fever lest the assault should be launched before the new arrangement was settled, but there was no need for this anxiety. The gun in the breastwork had opened fire again with round shot, and was resuming its remorseless monotonous pounding of the walls.

Jonquier left to Dupont the marshalling of the trembling civilians and went down again to the breach. The whole side wall was now blasted away, and was represented by a long heap of stones piled up from ground level. The sun was pouring into the long room, illuminating the chaos within – shattered furniture, huddled corpses, scattered stonework.

The firing was now being directed at the corner of the building, where the walls were trebled in thickness in a solid pillar to support the weight of the floors above. At every impact of a ball the building trembled, and they heard the fall of a little avalanche of stone outside. Jonquier wondered grimly what would happen when the pillar gave way. He looked out through the breach at where the gun was firing away, remorselessly, one shot every four minutes. There was only death or captivity in store for him if it continued. Yet there was no means of silencing it. Jonquier thought of a sally; he might gather the greater part of the garrison together and charge out and try to capture and damage the gun. But he put the project away as hopeless. There was no possible chance of it succeeding. Two hundred men could not charge across four hundred yards of open country against two thousand enemies. To attempt it would only precipitate the end. The only thing to do was to fight it out to the last where he stood – a determination which suited his temperament admirably. He set his teeth with sullen ferocity.

There was not much longer to wait. One last shot knocked away so much of the supporting pillar that it collapsed with a rending crash. The whole building was full of the sound of smashing rafters. Stones and plaster rained down from above as the whole angle of the building collapsed. The dust hung thick as fog round the fort. It seemed for a brief space that the whole structure would fall like a house of cards. The men at the loopholes on the first floor and on the roof were flung down as the floor heaved beneath them. Then with a horrid sound the bell tower which surmounted the angle buckled in the middle and came crashing down on to and through the roof, flinging the look-out sentry in a wide arc a hundred feet to the ground.

Jonquier wiped the blood from his forehead where it had been cut by a flying chip of stone, and peered through the dust.

'Stand to your arms, men!' he roared. 'Here they come!'

Masses of the enemy had broken out from their cover behind the mound, at the roadside, in the ditches. They were racing up the hill. Their wild yells reached Jonquier's consciousness as only a shrill piping – rage and excitement having forced up his blood pressure to such a pitch that his hearing played him tricks. His own stentorian shouts, the reports of the muskets, seemed to him no louder than the sound of children at play.

'Don't fire until you can see the buttons on their clothes!' he yelled. 'Aim low!'

But half his men were too numb and dazed to fire. Others loosed off their muskets at hopelessly long ranges. A solid wave of stormers reached the palisades and burst through the gaps. Only one or two fell to the firing. The others poured forward up to the breach and began to pick their way through the littered stones.

'Back with them!' yelled Jonquier.

With his blood aflame he leaped on to the breach. Somehow he had lost his shako, so that his sparse fair hair gleamed in the sunshine. He plunged down the ruins sword in hand, but none followed him. He struck someone down, and found himself in the midst of enemies. For yards on either side of him Spaniards were pouring up the breach. Some gathered round him, and he slashed at them impotently with his sword – an odd, ungainly figure he made with his pot belly, plunging about on the heaped stones, cutting at his wary enemies. He felt the blade rasp down a musket barrel. Then he became conscious that someone was shouting at him, the same word, over and over again. They were calling on him to surrender.

'Never!' he said, and slashed once more.

Ten yards away a Spaniard dropped on one knee and took aim. The musket cracked, and Jonquier fell on his face among the piled-up stones. His little short legs moved pathetically for a moment.

And the breach was won and La Merced was taken. The Spaniards raged through the corridors and the halls and the chapel. They were as merciless as only men can be who have taken a place by storm, as merciless as may be expected of men with uncounted defeats to avenge, with uncounted oppressions to make payments for. Some of the groups they met here and there tried to fight, and some tried to surrender, and each attempt was equally unavailing. The wretched French boys died on the bayonets, or were shot at close range so that the flash of the muskets scorched their clothes. They were hunted down in the cellars like rats. They were killed as they huddled round the chapel altar. They were flung over the parapets of the roof, and were finished off as they writhed with broken bones at the foot of the wall.

CHAPTER XI

So La Merced was taken, and the passage was won across the Orbigo. Great was the plunder. The cellars were heaped with food – there was enough there to supply the starving Spaniards for a week at least. There were chests of silver coin, the accumulated tribute wrung from unhappy Leon. There were clothes for the naked, and weapons for the unarmed. There was a six-pounder field gun to add to the artillery train of the besiegers, and there were welcome supplies of powder. And lying among the ruins, easily to be found, were the cannon balls that the siege gun had fired at the place. Some were in fragments and useless, but quite half were still round enough to be used again. Ninety rounds had sufficed to batter in the walls of La Merced, and there were still four hundred to load on to the ammunition mules.

And the wine, the vast barrels of last year's vintage, was a delight to these men, who for months had lived lives of severe hardship. It was not long before every nook and cranny of La Merced was filled with shouting quarrelling groups, who drank and fought and fell asleep and woke to drink again. The natural abstemiousness of the Spaniard and the peasant was forgotten in the flush of victory. By midnight three-quarters of the victorious army was dead drunk. The tiniest fraction of the French army would have won a resounding victory over them if such had been near, but there was none. There were some among the Spaniards who kept their wits – especially those who had first reached the treasure chests. They must have borne in mind the cry of the irregulars at the beginning of the war – '*Viva Fernando y vamos robando*' – 'Long live King Ferdinand and let's go robbing' – for during the night several little parties of men made unobtrusive departure from the fort, with heavy haversacks, which might have emitted the musical jingle of coined silver if they had not been so carefully packed. The disintegrating effect of victory upon undisciplined forces was thus early marked.

But the morning and the rising sun found at least the most important unit of the attacking force still at its post. The gun still stood in its redoubt, glaring motionless over the earthen parapet. The heavy timbers which had been laid beneath its wheels were splintered and cracked under the shock of the recoil of its ninety discharges. Heaped up beside it were cannon balls in depleted pyramids, opened barrels of powder, all the litter which the gun's crew had hastily left behind when they ran forward to join in the plunder of the fort. The commanding officers of the army, even, were not there. They were in a peasant's cottage a mile away.

It had been a deadly shot that Jonquier had fired, the one that had flicked those masses of earth from the parapet. Hugh O'Neill had received the full blast of pebbles and sand right in his face, driven with enormous force, as he had stood in the redoubt directing the fire. They had borne him away stunned; the quick blood had masked his face so that Carlos O'Neill did not know the extent of his brother's injuries, while he stayed to continue the battering, and to conduct the parley with the French commander, and to let his yelling hordes loose in the assault when the corner of the fortress collapsed. He did not know how badly Hugh was hurt until the afternoon, when he mounted his big horse and rode back to the cottage, intent on cheering his wounded brother with the news of the success.

Hugh was in no mood to be cheered by any news whatever. Consciousness had returned to him, and all he could think of was the agony in his face and eyes – his eyes were sightless pits of pain from the sand which had been flung into them. There were no medicines, no dressings. The men who were with him could only lave his ragged face with cold water and hold his arms when his hands sought in his madness to increase the damage done, while he screamed and choked with the pain, uttering horrid shapeless sounds from the tongue and through the cheeks that the stones had riddled, revealing the shattered stumps of the teeth the stones had broken.

He would have asked them to kill him and end his agonies, Carlos guessed, if he had been able to articulate, and more than once he thought of using the pistol in his belt on this brotherly duty, but he could not bring himself to do it. He could only sit there beside him, listening to the horrid sounds, until at last pain brought its own relief and Hugh fell unconscious again. Mortification and blood-poisoning might in the end save Hugh from his fate, of dragging on his existence blind and with a face no one could see without shuddering, a blinded officer, dependent until the end of his days upon charity.

The gun called insistently for all the attention Carlos could give. The blow must be struck hard and quick now that the way had been opened for it. There must be no dallying now. The French dominion over the plains must be shattered before they could draw together sufficient forces to parry the blow. Carlos had never been anything other than a soldier. His childhood had been passed in barracks, and his adolescence in the ranks. His father and his grandfather and his great-grandfather before him had been soldiers. Family tradition and the professional pride of the soldier by birth forbade him to think of abandoning his task. The possibility never occurred to him. His brother might die of disease or starvation, but he himself must go on. The government he served was notorious for its inefficiency and its ingratitude, but the soldier does not bear that in mind. He knew nothing, or next to nothing, of the peasants he wished to set free – the monasticism of barracks gave few opportunities to a soldier of meeting the people who found the money to clothe and feed him – but that was beside the point; it was as inconsiderable as the fact that he knew nothing of the men he was to kill. His sole task was to go on fighting. He was undoubtedly glad that the fortune of war had brought him his present important command instead of the obscurity of an artillery captaincy, just as in the old days he had been glad that Fate had given him the dignified occupation of man-killer instead of relegating him to the lowly ranks of farmers or doctors or shopkeepers, but this again had no influence on his decision to continue with his duty. Heredity and environment left him incapable of considering any other course. He must go on fighting as a river must run downhill.

So that in the morning the soldiers and the brigands who were sleeping off their debauch in and around La Merced were roused by their commander with bitter words. The lash of his tongue drove them back into the ranks, and set the teamsters hurriedly harnessing up the draught animals to the gun, and the muleteers loading their mules again with cannon balls and barrels of powder. The column was formed quickly enough, the Castilian lancers riding ahead, the infantry trailing along the road with no more trace of formation than a flock of sheep. They were over the river at last, pouring forward on to the rich plains, chattering and laughing and singing, while in their midst rode O'Neill on his huge grey horse. He was silent and dry-eyed, although he looked back to the cottage where his brother lay awaiting death in charge of the half-dozen lightly wounded. Behind came the gun, rumbling and clattering along the stony road, with its long team extending fifty yards ahead of it, and the attendant gunners walking at its side, while after it rambled the fifty pack mules of the ammunition train, with their balanced nets of cannon balls or barrels of powder rubbing their raw backs rawer still.

It was a typical day of the Spanish spring, with winter left behind. The sky was a hard blue, with scarcely a cloud, and the sun that glared down upon the plains bore more than a promise of its midsummer tyranny. As far as the eye could reach the plain rolled away on all sides in gentle undulations, green and pleasant now with the young corn, and only broken here and there by the scattered villages of greyish-brown brick.

Over the plain and into the villages the invasion swept like a flood. Urquiola and his lancers came clattering in.

Haughtily they made their demands. Who was there who had shown signs of acquiescing too readily in the French dominion? The villagers pointed to one and another whose fate was sealed. What carts, what draught animals were there? Each village must find food in proportion to its size, twenty loaves to every house, one sheep to every three, delivered immediately in the carts. Money? Communion plate? Powder and shot? All was swept in. Young men of military age? They must join the ranks. The liberation of the plains proceeded satisfactorily.

At the next river there was a force of the enemy, only half a company, a hundred men. They had no fort here to guard the bridge, there was only an entrenched redoubt covering the approaches, in which the garrison could retire on the approach of an enemy; normally the men lived in billets in the village. The garrison had taken refuge here the day before, as soon as they heard the noise of the bombardment of La Merced, like a minute gun proclaiming the end of the French dominion over the province of Leon.

They had no artillery and little food, and they knew that the message they had sent to the town of Leon asking for help would bring small response, and they had had a chilly night huddled in the trenches, and when they saw three thousand enemies pouring down the road towards them their hearts misgave them. Jonquier had died rather than yield; the elderly lieutenant in command here preferred to yield rather than die. He guessed what must have happened at La Merced, and when he saw the big gun run up and preparation made to batter a gap in his flimsy earthworks he had one of his white shirts hoisted on a pole in sign of surrender. He had a strong card to play. The bridge behind him was of wood. He would burn it unless their lives were spared.

O'Neill rode up to the redoubt on his grey horse, with his interpreter running by his stirrup, and granted the terms demanded without argument; time was valuable now. The garrison marched out feeling a little sheepish, and laid their arms on the ground while the Spaniards clustered round them. The French had been promised their lives, but they had been promised nothing else. They were stripped of most of their clothes, of their invaluable shoes, of their haversacks and pouches. Finally, half naked and barefooted, they were handed over to a sergeant to escort to the rear.

What their fate was to be was rather worse than the elderly lieutenant had ever contemplated. Ferrol was the nearest place where the Spaniards could lodge prisoners in security, and Ferrol was two hundred miles away, beyond the Cantabrian mountains. French prisoners, barefooted and half naked, guarded by men without the least interest in keeping them alive, would fare badly in a mountain march of two hundred miles through a hostile population. But they were fools, of course, to have expected anything better.

Then the column pressed on, over the wooden bridge. The Asturians and the Galicians, and the Navarrese whom Mina had sent, were prodigious marchers. The regulars – for what the name is worth – of the Princesa Regiment kept up as best as they could. The sun began to sink towards the west, behind them. Still they toiled on, down one long incline and up the next. Every little crest they reached displayed the same interminable landscape before them, in which the villages came as welcome but only transient breaks. Still they tramped along the narrow road, sandy here and rocky there, while the sun beat upon their backs and the dust caked upon their mouths, and O'Neill sat silent on his horse in the midst of them.

In the late afternoon there came a sudden flurry of excitement. One of Urquiola's lancers came riding up to the column, and the news he bore caused O'Neill to drive in his spurs and gallop forward hastily to the head of the line. There was cavalry out ahead of them; it might be

Kellermann's dreaded dragoons come up from Estremadura. The rumours that Leon was bare of troops save garrisons might be false. A thousand dragoons, led by the man whose charge had won the battle of Marengo, would sweep this flimsy infantry away, capture the gun, and bring this expedition to a ridiculous end.

However, O'Neill found his alarm unjustified. There was only a single squadron of French cavalry out on the plain; presumably they were the recruits with remounts whom report had described as detained in Leon on their way south. Urquiola's two hundred lancers hung round them, neither side daring to subject their shaky troops to the trial of a charge. O'Neill could see the French commander riding in front of his men, shading his eyes with his hand as he peered forward into the setting sun to ascertain what was this unexpected army pouring into Leon.

At sight of the French a yell of defiance went up from the marching infantry. The Spaniards shook their fists and waved their weapons, and called to their enemies to come on. At the sound O'Neill's lips wrinkled in a sneer, although he did not let his men see it. Three times already he had marched with Spanish armies which had yelled defiance at the sight of the enemy and which had called just as eagerly for battle. And every one of those three Spanish armies had been shivered into fragments at the first charge of the French cavalry – brave words forgotten, heroic determinations thrown away, weapons cast aside, running terrified in all directions. O'Neill had no illusions about the quality of this fourth army. Mina's disciplined Navarrese might stand firm. The others would run. He could only hope to achieve anything with this mob by the inglorious method of avoiding all collisions in the open country, attacking garrisons while he might and hurrying to the shelter of the mountains at the first approach of a field army.

The commander of the French cavalry, having noted

the length of the column on the road, and the gun and the wagons at the rear, and the bearing of the troops, and all else concerning which he would have to make report to his master, wheeled his men about and trotted off, Urquiola and his lancers trailing after him at a safe distance. And at the same moment the milk-white spires of Leon cathedral, tinged to pale rose in the reflected light of the sunset, showed at last upon the horizon. Not for two long years of war had any Spanish army – save those marching back to captivity in France – set eyes upon them. It was with some consciousness of achievement that O'Neill gave orders for the march to end, for pickets to be sent on up the roads while the men found shelter in billets or bivouacs where they could, and for the gun to be halted under his own supervision in the roadside inn which he decided should be his headquarters for the night.

CHAPTER XII

O'NEILL DINED that night in the company of his senior officers; el Platero sat at the foot of the table, uncouth in his stubby black beard – he never seemed to have more or less than four days' growth – and with him were the majors commanding the three battalions of the Princesa Regiment, and Don Cesar Urquiola, and Alvarez, who commanded the Navarrese, all of them light-hearted and gay. They ate the tough chickens with relish, and they drank the best wine the worried innkeeper could provide.

This latter individual fluttered round them anxiously. It was nervous work satisfying the wants of the new conquerors; the fact that there was not the least chance of his being paid for this dinner, or for the accommodation of the two hundred men who were billeted in the outbuildings, was the least of his anxieties. His inn had been a favourite rendezvous for young French officers riding out from Leon, who had even been known to pay for their meals, and he feared lest this should be held to indicate that he was a 'Josefino' – one who had become reconciled to Joseph Bonaparte's rule over Spain – and if that were the case his existence would end abruptly in a noose of a rope.

No wonder he did his poor best to see that his visitors were comfortable, and he eyed with increasing trepidation the stony melancholy of O'Neill, who sat heedless of the gaiety of his companions, drinking glass after glass of wine with no visible effect. The dim candlelight shining on his face showed his expression to be desperately unhappy. He looked out over the heads of his officers, and seemingly through the blotched white-washed walls into the darkness beyond. It was only that morning that he had left his brother blinded and with his face in tatters. And the Irish blood in his veins, small in proportion though it might be, made him specially liable to these fits of brooding melancholy.

Yet there were moments of satisfaction even during this nightmare depression. They came when his glance wandered out through the window, out to the courtyard lit by the lanterns of the headquarters guard. For there, solid and immovable in the centre of the court, stood the ponderous mass of the gun. O'Neill found something supremely comforting in its presence. He had come to love that colossal eighteen-pounder.

Outside, at the door of the inn, an argument arose. The sound of it drifted into the main room where the officers sat. They could hear men expostulating, and a deep booming voice, unknown to them, overriding the expostulations. Finally the door opened and a Franciscan friar entered. He was a huge, burly man; his hood fell back over his shoulders revealing a close-cropped head of black hair and a wild tangle of black beard. His greyish-brown robe was in rags so that his bare legs could be seen. His sandalled feet were filthy with road travel. Behind him were visible the frightened innkeeper and an equally frightened Jorge, who were responsible for admitting him.

The huge Franciscan – his head seemed to brush the low ceiling – gazed down at the men around the table, and addressed himself without hesitation to O'Neill.

'You are the general of the army?' he demanded.

'Yes,' said O'Neill.

'I have a message for you.'

O'Neill signed to Jorge to withdraw and close the door, but the friar checked him.

'It does not matter who hears my message,' he said. 'It is one of good cheer. Go up boldly against Leon. The walls will fall before you, and the atheists will die – will die – will die. The hand of God is at work in Leon, and those whom God may spare for *you* to kill must be killed without mercy. They were all killed at La Merced?'

'Yes,' said O'Neill.

'All? Every one? That is well. But you spared those others today at the bridge of Santa Maria. That is evil. The atheists must be slain, and you have spared a hundred of them to fatten in idleness.'

El Platero laughed; he knew – none better – how inappropriate a description this was of the prospective fate of the wretched prisoners sent back to Galicia. But his laugh ended on a wrong note as the Franciscan turned his terrible eyes upon him.

'The hand of God may reach those who laugh in the hour of the Church's agony,' said the Franciscan solemnly.

Then he looked deliberately at each person at the table, and each one dropped his eyes before his glance.

'Kill, and spare no one,' he said. 'Remember that the hand of God is at work in Leon. I am going on to be the instrument of God elsewhere.'

With that, he turned about. They heard him stride

94

down the little passage, and they heard him bless the sentry at the main door as he passed him.

'Who the devil is that?' asked el Platero.

'God knows,' replied Urquiola. 'Here, innkeeper, innkeeper!'

The worried host came in, wiping his hands nervously on his grey apron.

'Who was that friar?' snapped Urquiola.

'Really, sirs, I do not know for certain. They say —'

'Well?'

'They say that he was one of those that fought at Saragossa. Brother Bernard, the world calls him. They say he is more than human. A year ago Marshal Bessières at Valladolid offered a thousand dollars for his head, and as you see, gentlemen, he has not paid it yet. He was in the city of Leon for three weeks past. He walked in the streets, but the French did not arrest him. They say he can make himself invisible to French eyes, but I do not know whether that is true.'

'Neither do I,' said el Platero with grotesque solemnity.

'That will do, innkeeper,' put in O'Neill, unexpectedly, and the innkeeper withdrew relieved.

O'Neill sat brooding at the head of the table. Suddenly he looked up.

'Gentlemen, I hope you have enjoyed your dinner,' he said.

That was one way of dismissing them. El Platero remembered he had to go round the outposts to see that his men were awake. Urquiola had problems of forage and farriery to solve. The officers bade O'Neill good night; he hardly condescended a monosyllable in reply, still sitting there, with his hands resting on the table, looking into vacancy. They were all a little piqued at this aloofness, and grumbled at it as they emerged into the keen night air. The thought was in the minds of all of them that this boy of four-and-twenty had no business usurping the com-

mand over grown men of experience. They had not
minded obeying Hugh O'Neill, but this young Carlos. . . .
It was a pity he was the only artillery officer of them all.
Still, that did not make him entirely indispensable. The
men would follow him while he gave them victory and
plunder, but at the first check . . .

O'Neill, who had not slept for two nights, allowed his
forehead to droop down to the table. Among the three
thousand men whom chance had brought under his command there was not one to whom it occurred to see that
O'Neill had a bed to sleep in. The groom who had brought
in his saddlebags was now comfortably drunk in the cow-
stall where Gil was tethered. It did not occur to his Spanish
mind to seek out any additional duty. It was left to the
innkeeper to suggest bed to O'Neill, and to bring in a
sack of straw and lay it on the floor for him – the innkeeper
slept in the pleasant warmth of the kitchen, with his wife
and serving maid and ostler and five small children. Now
that Hugh O'Neill was disabled, there would be no one to
dress the wound which el Bilbanito's knife had made in
Carlos O'Neill's arm three weeks before. Fortunately a
clean stab heals best when bound up in the blood, so that
Carlos had no need now for the sling, and the wound itself
was nearly healed and hardly troubled him.

Yet O'Neill's night was disturbed. There were numerous people who urgently wanted to see him, people who
had somehow, despite guards and curfew orders, contrived
to escape from Leon and had walked or ridden out to
where, as rumour had soon spread the news, the headquarters of the raiding army were to be found. Most of
them were pitifully anxious to interview O'Neill. They
pressed actual gold – and gold was a very rare commodity
in Northern Spain at that time – into Jorge's hand to bribe
him into ushering them into O'Neill's room, and once
there they were ready to talk at incredible length. They
all had something to explain, they all sought to compen-

sate for past misdeeds. The Spanish interpreter to General Paris, Governor of Leon, wanted to explain why he had accepted this employment, and why he had translated Paris's brutal proclamations into Spanish. It was done with the most patriotic motives, he assured O'Neill, and in proof of it he was ready to tell O'Neill all he knew about the organization of the French garrisons in the province. The Mayor of Leon came out; he wanted to explain that he accepted office under the French occupation solely to be able to soften down the French demands upon his long-suffering people. Now he was delighted to be able to tell O'Neill all about the arrangements made for guarding the town in the event of a siege. There were other men most unjustly suspected of having favoured the French cause who were anxious to clear themselves of this charge by denouncing others – some of whom had already made their appearance at headquarters with reciprocal denunciations. Even the principal brothel keeper of Leon came with a plausible explanation of the hospitality offered to the army of occupation.

All night long there was a constant trickle of people out from the town, and O'Neill had to deal with them all. Delegation of authority is a difficult matter with an improvised army, and especially so when internal jealousies are present. O'Neill could leave the cavalry scouting to Urquiola, and the outpost work to el Platero – they could be relied on to do such work well. But it was a very different matter when it came to the business of a staff. The men who might be expected to do staff work well were not to be trusted at all in an army where anyone might hope to succeed to the command if he guided chance the right way. O'Neill was acutely conscious that he did not possess the gift, almost essential to a leader of irregulars, of making men love him. Unlike Hugh, who could crack jokes in Gallego and Asturian, and who won the hearts of everyone he met, Carlos could only speak his own Castilian and left everyone in his army indifferent as to whether he lived or died. He had to watch every move of his subordinates, and he had to lock within his bosom any information which came his way – and he had to reserve for himself, in consequence, the labour of gathering such information.

He was a good soldier, nevertheless. He knew what information he needed, and he did his best to acquire it. In two years of desperate warfare he had amplified the theoretical knowledge acquired from his father, and in barracks, and in the military college at Zamora. He knew just how much he could ask of his men and how far they could be relied on. Most important of all, he knew what he wanted to do and was utterly determined to do it. There would be neither divided counsels nor dilatory execution in the handling of O'Neill's army.

This was confirmed again the next morning, when an hour before dawn saw the invaders roused from their billets and assembled on the road; by two hours after sunrise Uquiola's lancers were prowling round the walls of Leon and the infantry were forming up in a mass outside the Benavente gate. General Paris within the walls was a wily old soldier. He had a thousand men under his command, and he knew well enough that it was an insufficient force to defend a long medieval wall against a serious attack and at the same time hold down a rebellious population of fifteen thousand or more. He intended to make his real defence within the citadel he had built up inside the town, but at the same time he had not the least intention of abandoning walls and city before he was sure that the attackers were capable of capturing them. He was not to be bluffed into yielding an inch prematurely.

It did not take long to convince him that the attacking force was in earnest and had the means to enforce their will. A column of troops, in the brown clothing which now indicated the Spanish regular army, marched off round to the east side of the town. Paris's telescope saw that they had scaling ladders with them. Meanwhile, up the road to the Benavente gate, he saw a big gun come lumbering up. His cavalry reconnaissance had made no mistake when it credited the invaders with siege artillery. The gun was brought up to within a quarter of a mile of the gate, and was swung round into position with the utmost deliberation. A train of mules followed behind with ammunition. Through his glass Paris could see an officer on a grey horse directing operations. Presumably that must be the O'Neill he had heard about.

Paris could do nothing to discommode the Spaniards while this was going on. He had no artillery at this point which could have the slightest effect. The flimsy medieval wall was not wide enough to bear big guns, even if he had any to spare, and even if the Emperor who had sent him into the country had condescended to supply him with them. He had two or three two-pounders – 'wallpieces' – but they were not accurate enough to have any effect at a quarter of a mile. The besiegers had chosen the weakest spot in the whole circumference.

O'Neill dismounted from his horse and straddled the trail of the gun. His target practice against La Merced two days before had given him an exact knowledge of the capabilities of the gun. It was a beautiful weapon, shooting with an accuracy which had surprised him, accustomed as he was to the rough and ready equipment of the Spanish regular artillery. As he looked along the sights he knew exactly where the shot would hit, and his expectation was fulfilled. The cannon ball crashed into the huge wooden gate exactly over the lock. The timber shattered in all directions. Methodically, O'Neill changed his target. Half a dozen rounds left the whole gate hanging in splinters. The gate had been built up with sandbags behind the timber, but sandbags could not be expected to stand long against eighteen-pound cannon balls hurled against them.

At every shot the shape of the heap changed, as the contents of torn bags at the bottom poured out and full ones from the top came rolling down. Before long the steep-sided mass of sandbags had degenerated into a mere mound, easy to climb and difficult to defend. O'Neill sent one of Urquiola's lancers flying to the Princesa Regiment with the order to attack. Alvarez drew his sword and ran to set himself at the head of his Navarrese. With a yell they all poured forward. To the right of the gate went el Platero; to the left Jorge led the other guerilleros. Their duty was to open musketry fire on the defenders of the wall while Alvarez burst through the gate with his solid column. Yet as they charged forward they saw spots of colour appearing on the top of the wall. Men up there were waving their arms, waving flags, waving scarves, dancing with delight. General Paris had withdrawn his garrison into the citadel in the nick of time. He was not going to try to defend that wall against an assault and an escalade with a furious civilian population at his back and only a thousand men all told.

CHAPTER XIII

THE SUCCESSFUL army poured through the steep and narrow streets. The population was mad with joy. Bright shawls waved from the windows. The streets were full of cheering mobs. The men clapped their deliverers on the back, and the women tore their arms and equipment from them and carried them themselves. Patriotic persons and those with guilty consciences rolled barrels of wine out to the street corners and stood with cups in their hands beseeching passers-by to drink. A bevy of women surrounded O'Neill, stroking the big grey horse, spreading scarves under his feet, kissing O'Neill's hands and even his boots and breeches if his hands were not attainable.

O'Neill was too preoccupied with urgent business to enter into the spirit of the thing. He had to shout his orders over the heads of the people to where Urquiola rode beside him. The half-dozen troopers who accompanied him went clattering off, each despatched on a separate errand. He was too much of a soldier to allow civilians to delay him when he had a course of action mapped out. The municipal deputation which came to meet him was heard with scant attention, and they pulled long faces when a few brief words in reply told them the number of shoes, and of suits of clothes, and the amount of solid hard cash the city was expected to contribute to the cause, and that within three days. Every householder must be ready to lodge and maintain two soldiers from now on, indefinitely. But O'Neill's final order excited a different kind of interest. There must be a scaffold and the municipal garotte erected within two hours in the Plaza Mayor, and the town executioner must be in attendance.

The news of the request sent a buzz of excitement round the town, for no Spanish fiesto could be really complete without a public execution; when the chapter of the Cathedral heard of it the arrangements for the celebration of the thanksgiving mass were abruptly cancelled; the clergy would not risk their dignity in hopeless competition with the spectacle.

O'Neill rode off to where, against the north wall, the garrison had concentrated to stand a siege. Leon could not boast a military citadel, like Burgos, but General Paris had done his best to compensate for the omission. The thick-walled prison and the town hospital stood side by side beyond the Plaza Menor in complete isolation; he had torn down, long before, one or two houses which offered points of vantage to any who might attack. He had built solid works connecting the two buildings and strengthening weak points. Here with a clear space all round him, with six weeks' provisions in his cellars, and four field guns to keep the mob at a distance, he felt confident that he could beat off any attack until the concentration of outlying garrisons or the despatch of some other army of relief should set him free again.

Paris would have felt happier in his mind if the guerilleros had not possessed a powerful siege gun – as was the case everywhere else, his arrangements had only envisaged a spasmodic attack by an enemy without artillery – but even as things were he felt few qualms. He had more troops and more guns than Jonquier had at La Merced, and an infinitely stronger fortress whose peculiar construction afforded several concentric rings of defence.

O'Neill, reconnoitring cautiously from an upper window of a house on the corner of the Plaza Menor, recognized the difficulties before him. He could breach those walls with the gun, doubtless, but one breach would not suffice. When that breach was won the gun would have to be brought up to it to breach the wall behind, and when the prison was finally taken there would still be the hospital. If the French fought with spirit there would be bloody fighting and tedious battering – weeks of it, presumably – before the whole place was taken. One gun would do its work so slowly, and in the progress of the siege there was always the chance – particularly at close quarters – of a lucky shot from the besieged, or a well-timed sally, disabling the gun completely. It would be a hard task to keep his wayward followers up to the effort and the self-sacrifice involved. If once they tired, or if he could not continually gratify them with success his army would fall to pieces. There was some excuse for the gloom which still clouded O'Neill's brow when he rode back; he bore too heavy a responsibility for a young man of twenty-four.

At the corner of the Plaza Mayor and the Rambla there were more women awaiting him. But these had not come to kiss his hands, or to spread shawls under his horse's feet. There were two or three small children, and a young and lovely woman, and one or two older women with white hair. They fell on their knees as he approached, and held out clasped hands to him. Unconsciously he began to rein Gil in as he neared them, but his ear caught a few words of their petition, and at once he loosened his reins and drove in his spurs so that Gil plunged forward again. They were asking for the life of a man; apparently they had discovered for whom the garotte was being prepared. O'Neill's black eyebrows came together, scowling. A young man with the fate of a kingdom in his hands, called upon to dispense the power of life and death, does not welcome arguments about his decisions. He had judged the men guilty, and they must die.

The young woman scrambled to her feet and ran and seized his arm, but he shook her off so that she fell on her face in the road, and the orderlies clattering behind him had to swerve to avoid her. He saw the white lips of the old women moving in prayer, but his ears refused to hear their words.

Alvarez and Captain Elizalde had done good work in the scant time allowed them, here in the Plaza Mayor. The scaffold and the garotte stood ready in the centre, with the executioner and his assistant gracefully at ease – the executioner was seated in the chair to which he would shortly bind his victims. On one side of the scaffold were the half-dozen drums of the Princesa Regiment; on the other, in a vivid mass were the clergy in their vestments with the Bishop at their head, ready to give their blessings and countenance to this display of justice. Round the sides of the square, and thronging the windows of the houses, were the population of the town – a thin line of soldiers prevented them from encroaching too near the scaffold.

Alvarez came up and saluted.

'Everything is ready,' he said. 'Shall I give the word?'

'Yes,' said O'Neill.

'There are one or two others,' said Alvarez, 'beside the ones you had arrested last night. The mob brought them to me, and the town council said they were traitors. I put them in with the rest.'

'Quite right,' said O'Neill, hoarsely.

Alvarez turned and waved his arm to a group of his men who stood, apparently awaiting his signal, round the portal of the Cathedral. They disappeared inside. In the beautiful Cathedral tower a bell began to toll, its deep note vibrating oppressively through the silence of the square. A procession emerged from the Cathedral door. Pablo Vigil, Alvarez's lieutenant, came first, strutting along much elated by the dignity and solemnity of the occasion. Then, three by three, came the victims and their guards, each man who was to die between two guerilleros. Some were old men and some were young; mostly they were of the type of portly citizen.

O'Neill recognized in most of them the men who had come to plead with him for their lives the night before. He remembered the arguments they had used, one after the other, and the bribes they had offered. Most of them had knelt to plead with him; some of them had wept when, after hearing all they had to say, he had called to the guard and had them locked up.

They had no dignity now, for Alvarez had stripped them to their shirts for greater shame. The wind flapped the garments round their thighs; one or two of them, unable to walk for weakness, were being dragged along by their guards. One of them was shrieking in a high treble. Round the square they went, right round to the Cathedral door again, and then out to the middle where stood the scaffold. The guards flung the first of them on to the wooden flooring, and the executioners fell upon him and hoisted him, nerveless but resisting feebly, into the chair. They made fast the straps, and clasped the iron collar round his neck.

The executioner applied himself to the lever, while Alvarez, his showman's instinct working double tides, signed to the drummers. To the roll of the drums the wretched man's limbs contorted themselves horribly within their bonds. It seemed as if all the thousands watching caught their breath simultaneously. The executioner put all his weight upon the lever and the screw broke the man's neck.

At that moment something crashed into the square, ploughing up the cobbles, and, ricocheting, crashed into the face of a house. The French were firing field guns from the citadel. There was panic in the square. The crowds of spectators began to push and struggle to get away; the soldiers broke their formation; the executioners hesitated in the midst of the business of taking the corpse out of the garotte. A flash of hope illuminated the features of the unhappy men waiting their turn to die. One of them actually, on his knees and with clasped hands, began to render thanks to God in a cracked voice.

A second cannon ball, pitching near where the first had fallen, intensified the panic. It seemed as if all Alvarez's carefully planned ceremonial was to be stultified. But O'Neill's voice, blaring like the bellowing of a bull, steadied the mob. He sat his horse rigidly in the centre of the square, keeping the big brute still while another shot fell only twenty yards from him. As he pointed out in his terrible voice, only a small part of the Plaza Mayor was exposed to the fire of the guns of the citadel. They were firing straight up the Rambla, and their shot could only reach the small portion of the square which lay in a direct continuation of this road. If the weak-kneed fools in that corner would only move – *quietly* – over to the other side of the square they would come to no harm and business could proceed.

So it was done. While one side of the square was deserted the crowds thronged the other three sides, and the executions went on with decency, the drums rolling, the bell tolling, and O'Neill on his horse like an equestrian statue watching the work being done.

This was as severe a blow to French rule of Spain as even the taking of La Merced. When the news of the executions at Leon went round no Josefino would feel himself safe. Every Spaniard would think twice before he made himself a tool of the usurper. French rule in Northern Spain could never be so secure in future. The knowledge was a source of satisfaction to O'Neill, but unhappily it is to be doubted if he had been entirely influenced by the need to achieve this result when he ordered the executions. Two years of savage warfare, the overwhelming responsibility of his position, the horrible wounding of his brother, and the present strain upon his nerves had brought out a vein of cruelty which had lain unsuspected within him. The mixture of blood which so often makes for cruelty may have been partly responsible as well, and at La Merced he had ample temptation to acquire the taste for slaughter. O'Neill on his horse was conscious of an inward delicious satisfaction at the sight of the contortions of the men in the garotte, even though he kept his face unmoved. It boded ill for the enemy he had to fight and for the people he had to govern.

With the conclusion of the killings and the approach of evening the city of Leon gave itself up to riot and revelry. During eighteen months of French occupation the people had been subjected to a severe curfew ordinance. The evening life of the streets in which the Spaniard takes so much delight had been denied to them, but now, with the French shut up in the citadel they could swarm here and there as they wished. They did not care that all the Rambla, from the Plaza Menor to the Plaza Mayor, was dangerous ground – the French sent a blast of grape up it whenever there were sufficient saunterers to justify the expenditure of a round of ammunition. They did not care that the peace of the evening was occasionally broken by musket shots, for the Navarrese were distributed in a semi-circle in the houses round the citadel and were taking long shots at any sentries who might be visible within. They did not care that the gun, wreathed incongruously in greenery by patriotic ladies, was being dragged by devious alleys to a corner where a working party under O'Neill's own supervision was toiling to build up solid the lower rooms of two houses to act as a battery for the bombardment of the morrow.

All the troops were not on duty. There still remained a thousand or two to join in the music and the dancing and light-hearted merriment, and to console those ladies whose husbands were at the wars, and to give pleasure to those others who were fortunate enough to have husbands who were careless or stupid. Anyone might have thought who saw the gay throngs that the war was over, that Spain was set free, instead of that a handful of irregular troops had gained a precarious hold over one little patch of the vast expanse of Spain. No one minded. No one could mind who for the first time for eighteen months was not compelled to go to bed at sunset. The night was all too short for them to wring all the pleasure they wanted out of its passing hours.

Even morning found them still gay. They demonstrated the ability of the Spaniard to make merry all night and still be able to face the day without depression. There was talk of a bull-fight. The aged, patriotic and wealthy Conde de la Meria was rumoured to have sent out of the town in search of bulls which Don Cesar Urquiola's Castilian gentlemen could ride down with their lances in accordance with the high tradition of Spanish chivalry – the day of the professional bull-fighter on foot was not yet come, by half a century.

A few of the more military minded and inquisitive among the inhabitants wandered down to the alleys round the Plaza Menor to see what was being done in the matter of the siege of the citadel. They found the soldiers busy barricading the alleys, knocking loopholes in walls, making ready to beat back the sorties which O'Neill judged would be launched upon them as soon as the big gun should open fire. To capture or disable that gun the French would pour out their blood like water.

He himself had hardly slept again that night. He had lain down and dozed in snatches now and then in the midst of the working parties. The lower rooms of the two houses he had selected were now filled with earth; the gun had been dragged into the narrow passage between them and earth had been heaped round it so that only its muzzle protruded, concealed as far as might be. At a hundred yards – the range which circumstances dictated – even the light guns of the garrison might disable this, the only siege gun at his disposal.

His heart almost misgave him when he looked out at the massive defences he had to penetrate, the palisades and earthworks and walls, the ditches and escarpments. He remembered with bitter amusement the words of Brother Bernard – 'Go up boldly against Leon – the hand of God is at work in Leon.' Brother Bernard could not be very well versed in siege warfare. There was no chance even of starving out the French, for O'Neill knew that General Paris had filled the cellars of the citadel with food long before. Many people had pressed upon him information regarding the stores there. They had counted the barrels of flour, and the tubs of salted meat, and the sacks of grain, and the barrels of wine which had been accumulated there during the occupation. It was the Spaniards who had had to make up that store; there were people in the town who had had to labour in the milling of the flour. And while the hundred and fifty thousand rations were being accumulated in the citadel the French had lived on further rations drawn from the luckless countryside. There was not the least chance that the stores might turn out to have been depleted by rash indents upon them to save trouble. Why, before O'Neill's very eyes arose the smoke of the French fires, cooking their morning soup. The two tricolour flags flaunted themselves from the flagstaffs at each end of the long fortress. O'Neill set his teeth and turned away to supervise the completion of the arrangements for the siege. He saw no sign of the hand of God being at work.

By noon he had everything ready. The gun was ready to open fire; its ammunition was hidden away behind masses of earth where no stray shot could find it out. Close at hand a hundred men stood with trusses of straw. These were to be thrown into the prison ditch when an assault was made, after the palisades had been shot down and a breach battered in the west wall of the prison. How many casualties would be incurred even if the attack succeeded O'Neill did not like to consider – and the greatest success which could be anticipated could only result in the capture of one-twentieth of the citadel. All the open space of the Plaza Menor would have to be crossed under a fire of point-blank musketry and of grape and canister from the artillery. But still, these losses would have to be faced. Perfectly conscious of what would be the result to him of a severe check, O'Neill went down to the gun to open fire.

The noise of the gun in that confined space was appalling. O'Neill and the gun team felt as if their heads were being beaten open with sledge hammers every time the gun went off. But the practice was good. A few rounds of grape tore a huge gap in the palisades, and then O'Neill began with round shot on the angle on the hospital. He would not direct his fire upon the main gateway, as the approach there was exposed too much to cross fire, and he shrewdly expected that within the courtyard, unseen, lay a field gun crammed with canister trained upon the entrance. He preferred to attack a spot not so easily defended. Round after round crashed against the wall. The bricks flew at every blow, but owing to the angle of impact it took some time before any hole was apparent in the wall.

It was strange that so little return fire was directed upon the gun by the defenders. There was a light gun in an embrasure some way down the wall from the point of attack, but it only fired twice, and each time the aim was dreadfully bad. The shots only brought down a shower of bricks from the face of a house twenty yards from the gun. O'Neill could not understand the reason for this silence. A further shot from the big gun brought down a little cascade of bricks from the angle of the wall. O'Neill left the gun for a moment, and went up to the first floor of the house beside it in order to inspect the progress of the bombardment without having his view impeded by smoke.

There seemed to be no sign of life in the citadel. Then suddenly he noticed that one of the two tricolour flags was invisible now. Someone must have hauled it down. As he looked, wondering, he saw the ponderous hospital gate swing open. He rushed back down the stairs shouting to his men – the anticipated sortie must be about to be delivered. Yet so quickly did he move, that by the time he was on ground level again it was only half open.

But no stream of soldiers yelling, 'Vive l'Empèreur' appeared. There was a distinct pause while O'Neill stood and wondered. Then someone came staggering out round the gate. He walked unsteadily a few yards towards the gap in the palisades and fell down. After him came a few more men, reeling and tottering. One of them, walking like a blind man, fell with a crash over the recumbent figure, and made no attempt to rise. Another suddenly doubled up with pain, sat down, and then fell over on his side. Not one of the group succeeded in reaching the palisades. The wondering O'Neill, completely puzzled, suspected a trap and yet, unable to see wherein it lay, stepped out into the open. He strode forward across the open space, and his men began to follow him. Not a shot was fired from the citadel. O'Neill pressed forward through the broken palisades, and reached the men writhing on the ground. He could gain no enlightenment from them. He went on, sword in one hand and pistol in the other, through the gate, and under the *porte cochère*, into the courtyard.

Here the sight presented to his gaze was horrible. The courtyard was heaped with men in the last stages of agony. They lay here and there raving in delirium, torn with pain, vomiting and retching. Some were dead, and they seemed the most fortunate. A field gun, just as he had expected, stood defiantly in the centre of the court facing him, but its crew lay dead around it. The guerilleros would take no further step forward; they clustered about the gate peering into the yard; most of them were praying and crossing themselves.

O'Neill shook off his superstitious fears. Alone, he opened the door beside him, and entered the building. The long room in which he found himself seemed full of groans and cries, and as his eyes grew accustomed to the lessened light he saw more men in agony writhing under the loopholes, and throughout the citadel he found more tortured humanity – dying men on the staircases, dying men on the parapets, dying men everywhere.

As Brother Bernard had promised, the hand of God had been at work in Leon – or rather, the white arsenic which he had caused to be mixed with the flour of the garrison's stores had had its effect.

CHAPTER XIV

THE LEONESE knew pity. When they heard the news they came, men and women alike, to try and care for the unhappy men whose bowels were being seared and torn by the poison within them. But arsenic knows no pity. It slew and slew and went on slaying. Many of the men who did not die at once survived only a few days, lingering until the secondary effects of the poison extinguished the flickering life in their wasted bodies. Only a few score of the garrison survived, bent and crippled. It had been a most notable slaughter, redounding to the credit of Brother Bernard. If a few more patriotic Spaniards would arise who could kill a thousand Frenchmen apiece the invasion of Spain would end abruptly.

But the fall of Leon, the capture of the citadel, was an event which was of first-class importance in the course of the war. At the news of it the whole province shook off its sullen fear of the French and took up arms. Every village contributed its band of half-armed irregulars; it was a rising more violent even than the one which had opened the war – the one which Bessières had extinguished in blood two years before. The other small garrisons scattered through the province were forced to take shelter within their little fortresses, round which prowled the rebels in their thousands, unable to do any harm to the stone walls, but watching and waiting, with the patience of wild animals and the same thirst for blood.

Nevertheless, these peasants had a proper respect for the outward signs of authority, and when a glittering cortège, all hung with orders and dazzling with gold lace, rode down from the mountains of Galicia and across the plains of Leon, it was received everywhere with deference. The horsemen who composed it seemed to be in a hurry to reach the city of Leon, and they rode fifty miles along the sandy roads with hardly a halt, clattering up to the town and through the gates with all the pomp and dignity they could display. They drew up outside the palace of the Conde de la Meria, where soldiers lounged before the doors.

'Go and tell Captain O'Neill,' said the leader to one of

them, 'that the Duke of Menjibar, Captain-General of Leon, has arrived.'

The soldier made his leisurely way into the palace, and the horsemen sat waiting in their saddles. They had to wait a long time; there seemed to be no great hurry to welcome the Captain-General of Leon or to offer him the subservience which his rank demanded. It was only after a considerable pause that the doors opened and O'Neill emerged. He was still wearing his shabby artillery uniform, but he bore himself very erect. His black eyebrows nearly met above his blue eyes – a danger signal to any who knew him. He took time to walk down the steps and out to where the Duke of Menjibar fumed in his saddle.

'There is some mistake,' said O'Neill slowly. 'Perhaps the message was delivered to me incorrectly. I know of no Captain-General of Leon.'

The Duke of Menjibar was a stout little man with fierce black moustaches. He beat impatiently on the pommel of his saddle.

'I am Captain-General of Leon,' he said. 'Do you doubt my word?'

'I doubt either your word or your sense,' said O'Neill.

'I hold the commission of the Junta,' said the duke. 'Must I show it to you to be believed? It will go hard with you if you compel me to.'

'From the Junta of Galicia?' asked O'Neill. 'There is no Junta of Leon, nor has been for two years back.'

'The Junta of Galicia represents Leon as well,' said the duke.

'Oh,' said O'Neill. 'So that discredited gang, loitering at Ferrol a hundred miles from the enemy, presume to nominate a captain-general for a province it has never set eyes on? I suppose it wants some of the gold we have captured? Or it wants to filch the credit for the conquest of Leon?'

'That is not the way to speak to me, Captain O'Neill. Remember, there are grave charges against you already.

Do not add to them.'

'Charges?' repeated O'Neill, innocently. 'Against me?'

'Don't try to fool me any longer,' said the duke, testily. 'Leave —'

O'Neill's gesture interrupted him. He glanced up at the windows of the palace whither a wave of O'Neill's hand had directed his gaze, and his words died on his lips. At every window there were soldiers, and every soldier had a musket, and every musket was pointed at the duke and his followers.

'I have a further message for you from the Junta,' said the duke hastily, playing the last card of his instructions. 'In recognition of your services the Junta is pleased to ignore the charges of mutiny preferred against you by Colonel Casa Riego. They will be glad to promote you to the rank of major-general, and they will solicit for you from the Central Junta at Cadiz the Order of Carlos III and the title of Conde de la Merced. That is, if I am able to report to them your willingness to act under my orders.'

O'Neill's smouldering anger burst into a blaze.

'You try to threaten and you try to bribe,' he blared out. 'I won't hear another word! Come down from your horse, you poor thing. Come down, or by God —! And you others, come off your horses! Here, Jorge, take them away. Put them in the dungeons under the prison. Set Vadilla and fifty men on guard over them. By God, you fools, I have it in mind to cut off your noses and ears and send you back to your Junta to tell them what I think of them. Perhaps tomorrow I shall do so – you can wait till then. With your stars and your epaulets, and you've never set eyes on an enemy in your lives. Jorge, take the horses away, too. We need remounts.'

This was treason of the wildest sort. The news that their Captain-General had been clapped into a dungeon would rouse the Galician Junta to transports of rage beyond even those caused by the defection of the Princesa Regiment.

114

Yet O'Neill did not stop there. Even before the keys were turned upon the raging Duke of Menjibar and his suite he sent messengers to summon the great men of the city. Coldly, he invited them to elect a Captain-General for Leon, and coldly he accepted the office which they hastened to proffer him. With rolling of drums and blaring of trumpets the city bailiff proclaimed him Captain-General of Leon, and the printing presses were set to work reproducing his decrees.

That was not the only function which Plaza Mayor witnessed during the hectic five days following the fall of the citadel of Leon. There were more Josefinos routed out from their hiding places, to be garotted with great ceremony on the scaffold in the centre of the square – scaffold and garotte stood there permanently now. From the surrounding country others were sent in, too. The peasants of the plains turned fiercely upon all who had shown any sign of approval of the French occupation. Day after day little groups of prisoners were brought into the city, and a word from O'Neill sent them to death in the square.

He never thought of trying them, of hearing what defence they might advance. The mere fact that they were brought to his notice, that they crossed his path, made them worthy of death. His pride, his sense of power and of his own importance, were swelled to monstrous proportions. He held the unquestioned power of life and death over a wide province, and the knowledge maddened the young man like a drug. His cruelty grew with its indulgence. That threat of his to the Duke of Menjibar about cutting off noses and ears was the smoke which indicated the fire beneath. His imagination was dark with mental pictures of horrible public tortures. It was only for five days that the carnival of death went on in Leon, but those five days are still spoken of with lowered breath in the city, and are remembered even though the cruelties of the Carlist wars and of the revolutions are forgotten.

Perhaps this knowledge of the impermanence of his position helped to madden him. It could only be a question of days before the French could collect an army which would sweep him back into the mountains, where his army would break up again perforce into fragments, where he would be relegated to the humble position of guerillero chief with perhaps a hundred followers – and they none too loyal – and where the Junta of Galicia could call him to account for his actions. The thought of it brought the blood to his skin and set him vibrating with rage, so that he wished, like Caligula (of whom he had never heard) that all the world had but one neck, which he could sever at a stroke.

The other garrisons of the province had to be reduced, and that was clearly the work of the Captain-General. Especially so, seeing that to do this called for the use of the big gun, and the possession of that gun was the outward sign of the lordship of Leon, like a king's sceptre. After five days in Leon, five days of executions and confiscations and requisitions, O'Neill marched out again. He took his army with him, and his big gun. He left behind him his puppet council; for he could not trust his army save under his own eye, while he knew there was not the slightest chance of those terrified civilians doing anything to thwart him.

There were only six small places which held out against the Spaniards in Leon, small fortresses guarding strategical points, after the fashion of La Merced and Santa Maria. The garrisons knew the details of the revolt; they had been brought by terrified Josefinos flying to them to take refuge. They knew how every soul in La Merced had been killed, and how the citadel of Leon had fallen, and how every man for miles round was in arms against their dominion again, and how O'Neill was a devil in human form, with an insatiable thirst for blood, and with a siege gun of unbelievable power and accuracy. They were cowed by the news before ever O'Neill came up against them. Santa Eulalia surrendered the moment that O'Neill appeared before it, and Mansilla and Saldaña and Carrion as soon as the big gun began to pound their flimsy defences to pieces. Each place was sacked in turn, and the French prisoners were sent back to Galicia – Heaven knew what chance they had of ever reaching it, and of being sent across the sea to the sybaritic comfort of the English hulks and of Dartmoor Prison.

Old General Dufour held out in Benavente for two whole days; he had a garrison of five hundred men and two concentric rings of defence. But he had no luck. If he had succeeded in beating back an assault he might have taken the heart out of the besiegers, but the wild attack of the peasantry and of the guerilleros lapped over his walls and up through the narrow breach. Dufour died sword in hand at the last breach, as Jonquier did, and his men died in holes and corners as the attackers raged through the place.

O'Neill left the place behind, silent, peopled only by the dead, and passed on with the big gun lumbering behind and the peasants flocking to join him. His circular tour had consumed less than a fortnight. In thirteen days he was back in Leon, marching his army in triumph through the cheering streets, and dragging behind him the wretched Spaniards who had been found in the captured places; men and women, peasants and landowners, tailors and cobblers, prostitutes, mistresses, and wives. Leon gave it-self up to a fresh orgy of blood and pleasure.

When they forgot to rejoice the Leonese found plenty at which to grumble. O'Neill had ten thousand men at his command now that he had swept the countryside. These ten thousand men had all to be fed and clothed and paid. O'Neill considered that the well-being of his soldiers weighed far heavier in the scale than the suffering of the civilians. Only the best – if there was enough of it – would do for his men, the best boots, the best clothing, meat every day although before they became soldiers they had rarely eaten meat oftener than once a fortnight. Anyone with a little hoard of money or silver plate was compelled to make a free gift of it to the State, which meant to General O'Neill. There was still some to be found despite the exactions of the French, and O'Neill had little difficulty in discovering it, for his reign of terror produced the inevitable crop of informers. Even the French had not thought of garotting the man who buried his spoons, but then the French could not call such an act 'treason', as O'Neill did.

In the forcing heat of present conditions all the characteristics of a military autocracy developed instantly; the inevitable bloodthirsty leader, trusting no one, with an eye on every department of State and a toadying mob of informers to help him; the usual inner ring of personal guards – lately the bands of Hugh O'Neill and el Bilbanito; the usual soldiery, rapidly learning their power and steadily increasing their demands; the usual ruined civilians, too terrified to murmur openly. In three weeks the government of Carlos O'Neill had reached the pitch which it took Imperial Rome a century to attain.

Possibly O'Neill was the only one of his army with an acute sense of the impermanence of it all. He was aware every minute that by now the French armies would be making a convulsive effort to gather together enough troops to strike him down. Wellington might be loose in the south, hot in pursuit of Massena's army reeling back from the lines of Torres Vedras, Soult might be staggering under the fearful blow dealt him at Albuera, King Joseph at Madrid might be trembling on his throne, but all the same they would spare no effort to dispose first of this menace to their communications. Every man that could be collected would be hurled upon him soon, and O'Neill, unlike his men, had not the slightest doubt as to the result.

Characteristically, he went forward to meet his fate, instead of waiting for it to come to him. Moreover, his best policy was to advance. A rebellion on the defensive is doomed for certain, as his military instinct assured him. Perhaps if he were enormously lucky and enormously active, if he rushed upon the great royal road which ran through Burgos and Valladolid, he might burst in among his enemies and prolong the struggle long enough for something unexpected to turn up and save him. Any other policy, whether he chose to wait round about Leon or to try to lead his forces back over the Cantabrian mountains to reduce the French garrisons along the Biscay coast, meant ultimate certain ruin.

There is room to doubt whether it was these considerations which influenced him in his decision to advance. O'Neill was a fighting man. His whole instinct called upon him to rush upon his enemies, to meet his fate halfway, to go down, if go down he must, with his face to the foe rather than his back.

CHAPTER XV

TEN THOUSAND men were on the march towards the Royal Road. O'Neill's messengers had summoned them from their billets in the town, and from their cantonments in the villages round about. Not even O'Neill, fount of dynamic energy though he was, had been able to make an army out of them. There was some faint trace of organization; there were the battalions of Mansilla and Saldaña; there were the first and second and third of Leon, officered somehow by untrained local magnates. Alvarez' band and el Platero's band and O'Neill's band had absorbed all the recruits they could, and more. Don Cesar Urquiola had five hundred cavalry now under his command, mounted on horses captured or requisitioned. But it was much more of a mob than an army.

The very act of concentrating on a single road had led to incredible muddles. Units approaching by by-roads had found their paths blocked by others marching across them, and, sooner than wait, had casually intermingled with the other stream. Some had been late and some had been early. The mass that poured down the road displayed no trace of military organization, despite the cavalry out ahead and the train of artillery in the rear, the six field guns, and the one big siege gun, and the long files of baggage mules. Handling ten thousand men is a very different matter from handling two thousand, and when the greater part of the ten thousand is a mere undisciplined rabble the task calls for a genius, which was exactly what O'Neill was not.

The fates turned against him. The pleasant spring weather which had prevailed for some time now changed on the very day that the march began. It seemed as if winter had come back again. A cold wind blew from out of the mountains, and it brought with it torrents of icy rain – the kind of rain which can only be experienced in Spain. The road was churned into mud, the ditches overflowed, the wretched soldiers were soaked to the skin. The end of the day's march found them only ten miles from the city, and many of the men went off in the night to seek the comfort of their homes. Of the remainder few were fortunate enough to have a roof over their heads, and spent a comfortless night lying out in the drenching rain.

And the next day it rained, and all night too, and all the day after; and by this time the eternal commissariat difficulty had arisen again. O'Neill had depended – for lack of any better system – upon supplies gleaned from the district over which they were marching, but it had been plundered and re-plundered, and when the news of the approach of the vast column was passed round, everyone fled from its path as if it bore the plague with it. Three days of rain and two of half rations made even that contingency not unlikely. The effect upon O'Neill was bad indeed. He raged against the delays and the desertions. The evil temper which the blinding of his brother and the responsibilities of his position brought him vented itself in unpleasant ways. He rode his big horse up and down the column and struck at the men with his whip, and they did not love him for it. The townsmen among them, and even the long-suffering peasants, did not take kindly to blows. But with the rain soaking his clothes and the icy wind whistling round him he could not control his temper, even if it had been possible after his weeks of enjoyment of un-fettered power.

A mile behind the rear of the columns he found the big gun stuck in the mud, buried up to the axles of its five-foot wheels, and Jorge and the rest of el Bilbanito's band toiling to free it. They were all free to work on this one gun, because the others had already been abandoned. It might have been more sensible to leave the heaviest behind and press on with the lightest, but it would not have been in accordance with the tradition of this army. Moreover, with further sieges in prospect, it really would not have been wise to abandon the big gun; they could manage with-out field guns, but not without the big eighteen-pounder. That was only an academic argument, all the same. No one would have dreamed of abandoning the gun which was the emblem of their new power and future hopes.

Yet they were having a difficult time; the draught mules floundered in the mud unable to gain a foothold, with the steam of their exertions rising from them in clouds, while Jorge and his men slaved with levers and drag-ropes to get the gun on the move again. They countered O'Neill's imprecations with dumb insolence and with angry mutter-ings, according to their several constitutions. Jorge wiped the blood from his neck where O'Neill struck him, but said no word. His mouth still smiled – his mouth was made for smiling – but his brow was black with anger. Someone shouted a curse after O'Neill when he wheeled the grey horse round again and galloped off amid a spatter of mud, but the wind and the rain deafened O'Neill's ears and dulled his senses so that the curse passed unheard and the man's life was not imperilled.

At midnight that night O'Neill in his headquarters in an inn shouted for the guard, and Jorge came in – circumstances and recent history had imposed upon the combined bands of el Bilbanito and O'Neill the two rôles of siege artillerymen and headquarters guard, with Jorge as general factotum. Jorge, looking round the room, was able to amplify from observation what he had guessed from the loud quarrellings he had heard through the door. O'Neill, white with rage, was seated at a small table at one end of the room; the candlelight lit up his face and revealed the ungovernable rage which distorted it. The other officers were standing here and there about the room, some of them sullen, some of them uneasy, but all of them obviously as angry as O'Neill himself, even if through fear or caution they could not show it. Clearly O'Neill had been dealing out reprimands regarding the marching, and clearly they had been resented.

'Arrest that man!' said O'Neill in a high-pitched voice.

The wild gesture of his arm indicated el Platero, standing mute and solitary in the middle of the room, with his usual four days' beard disfiguring his cheeks. There was a cornered look in his eyes, and he looked here and there sidelong, his hand on his knife. The other officers moved restlessly.

'Arrest him!' repeated O'Neill, his voice rising even higher in the scale. 'Lock him up. I shall have him shot.'

Jorge stood fast. With one hand he felt the weal on his neck where O'Neill's whip had drawn blood that afternoon. He was slow of thought, was this big-limbed boy, and when he thought his lips pouted in a rather inane grin.

'Don't stand grinning there,' snapped O'Neill. 'Take

him and put him under guard until morning.'

Jorge still stroked his neck. He had arrested many people already at O'Neill's bidding, and sometimes he had made history thereby – the Duke of Menjibar, and the pitiful men who had come out from Leon the day after La Merced fell, and men in Leon whom O'Neill had deemed to be traitors; men who had struggled and men who had wept, and women, too. He had obeyed because it had never occurred to him to do anything else. But now something else had occurred to him, and the pleasure of reaching a decision broadened his grin.

The others saw his face, and their attitude changed suddenly. They all seemed to draw in a little, ringing O'Neill round like dogs round a wolf. Still no word was spoken until O'Neill broke the silence.

'Why, what is this, gentlemen?' he asked. Bewilderment was taking the place of rage. His voice rang flat now instead of sharp.

El Platero laughed with the relief of tension, but it was left to Urquiola to express the changed views of the assembly. He stepped forward towards O'Neill, resting his fingertips on the table. His spurs rang in the silence. They even heard the creaking of his long gaiters of soft leather reaching up to mid-thigh.

'El Platero will *not* be shot,' he said. 'He will not be arrested.'

Now, too late, O'Neill tried to reassert his authority.

'Is this mutiny?' he roared, glaring round the room.

But in those few seconds the baseless fabric of his omnipotence had fallen to the ground, and nothing could build it up again. Everyone had realized that there was no need for anyone to obey him – at least as long as Jorge commanded the guard and Jorge was unfaithful to him. His choice of words, even, was unfortunate, for it put into the mouths of the others words which they might have flinched from using.

'Yes, it *is* mutiny,' said el Platero, and that clinched the matter.

Captain Elizalde sidled up alongside O'Neill and took his sword from his sheath, and the two pistols where they had lain handily on a shelf behind him, O'Neill offering no resistance in his surprise. Only when they were out of his reach did he think of falling sword in hand upon these mutineers and slaying them where they stood; now it was too late.

'Well, gentlemen, what shall we do with him now?' asked Urquiola.

'Keep him to work the gun,' said Alvarez – a surprisingly rash suggestion from one so experienced and cautious.

'Never!' said el Platero. 'You'll not risk my neck like that. Hang him and save trouble.'

'Hang him,' said one of the infantry majors, whom O'Neill had insulted before his men yesterday.

The candles flickered in a draught, casting strange shadows on O'Neill's face as he stood there, stock still, listening to this debate over his life or death.

Don Cesar pulled at his thin, old-fashioned beard, looking from one to the other.

'Can he hurt us if we set him free?' he asked mildly.

'Certainly he might,' said el Platero. 'I'll not trust him. Remember how his brother brought Princesa over to him. He might get us in his power again. Think what he would do to us then – look at his face.'

At el Platero's gesture they looked at O'Neill's face as none of them had dared up to that moment, and all of them caught the tail end of the expression which had flickered over it. At the thought of the treatment he would like to deal out to them O'Neill had been unable to keep his face immobile; the mental picture had swept away his stunned apathy.

'Hang him, I say,' said el Platero, rubbing in his lesson.

'Send him back to Leon,' suggested Major Volpe. 'They

know how to use the garotte there.'

Several people brightened at that suggestion, because the majority were not at all anxious to risk the obloquy which might reasonably follow the execution of the man who set Leon free.

'You cannot be sure they would use it on *him*,' persisted el Platero. 'Though there would be a few who would be glad to.'

'To Ferrol, then,' said Volpe. 'The Junta wouldn't hesitate.'

El Platero shook his head.

'Too far,' he said. 'Too risky.'

Don Cesar interposed again, mildly:

'What about the gun, gentlemen? Artillerymen are scarce.'

'I can work the gun,' said Jorge. Those were actually the first words he had spoken since O'Neill had called him in; up to that time his silence had made history, and now this brief speech of his obviously threw much weight into the scale.

The others looked at Jorge; they were trying to decide if here was another O'Neill, if by entrusting the gun to him they would be setting a new yoke on their necks all impatient of authority. They could not believe it of this thick-limbed, stupid boy who had forgotten his own surname.

'Of one thing I am sure,' said el Platero. 'I have never yet wanted to bring back to life any man I have hanged, but twice at least I have regretted allowing a man to live. I don't want this to be the third time.'

El Platero was clearly of a more thoughtful and philosophic turn of mind than his appearance would lead one to expect, but then he was older than most of them, and had worked at a highly skilled trade before ever he had become a guerillero.

'What would the men say?' asked Alvarez.

'Mine would not ask questions. You know best about your own. As for the others – if O'Neill is dead before we leave this room what would they care? What could they do? But if we let him go out from here alive, by this time tomorrow we may all be rotting on trees – if there are enough trees in this God-forgotten plain.'

'He would have to answer for my life to Mina,' said Alvarez.

'Mina? Do you think he cares about Mina? Mina is in Navarre, and we are on the borders of Castile.'

'Why not ask O'Neill what he has to say?' put in Delgado, the junior major of the Princesa Regiment.

'Yes,' said Elizalde eagerly.

All eyes turned towards O'Neill again, where he still stood at the table. He had listened almost unbelievingly while they bandied back and forth the pros and cons which would decide whether he should live or die. It was hard for a man to realize that one minute after being undisputed Captain-General of Leon he was in the most pressing imminent danger of dying a criminal's death. But Jorge had never taken his eyes off him, nor his hand from his knife.

O'Neill could only stammer at first. He may have wanted to plead for his life, but he could not do so. It was difficult to find his tongue in the face of this startling change in his position. It was Hugh O'Neill who ought to have met this situation, not Carlos – but Hugh would never have allowed matters to reach this pitch.

'He has little enough to say, you see,' sneered el Platero, 'this Captain-General.'

Jorge took a step forward.

With a huge effort O'Neill pulled himself together. He glanced like a hunted animal from one face to the next, and he found small comfort there. It was their lives or his, and O'Neill knew it too well. He could not gloss over that obvious fact in a ready speech for he was a man of no words. He could not promise amnesty and forgiveness so as to get himself out of that room to where he could change his mind safely, although possibly a man of glib tongue and no scruples might have persuaded the assembly to agree. He was a man of action, not of words. Finding himself in a trap, his whole instinct was to struggle madly, hopelessly even, like an animal. His fingers closed upon the top of the table in front of him; it was a small, massive piece of furniture, clumsily made out of thick slabs of wood. With it he could dash out brains, smash bones, hack his way to the door. At the prospect of action the fighting madness inflamed in his veins. He tightened his grip on the table, tautened his muscles, made ready to spring.

Jorge uttered an inarticulate shout of warning just as O'Neill charged. Like the fighting animal he was, O'Neill was guided by his instincts to launch himself upon the decisive point. Whirling the table horizontally to save time, he struck Jorge to the floor before the knife was well out of Jorge's belt. Then with incredible agility and strength he shifted his grip upon the clumsy weapon so that he held it by the legs and could make use of its heavy top. Don Cesar Urquiola caught him by the belt from behind as he went by; he tore himself loose and plunged for the door. Someone fired a pistol and missed; in the low narrow room the report sounded like a cannon. Elizalde barred his way; the table top crashed down on his shoulder and felled him. Delgado was before the door with his sword in his hand. O'Neill struck at him, but the table caught on one of the low beams of the ceiling. He struck again and dashed him out of his path. He was reaching for the door-handle, when Jorge flung himself along the floor like a snake and gripped his ankle. O'Neill and the table fell together to the floor on top of Delgado and Jorge and Elizalde. Their bodies tossed and heaved in a wild wrestling match. El Platero rushed in with knife

drawn, but before he could strike effectively a fresh up-
heaval engulfed him and he, too, fell to the ground en-
tangled in the struggling bodies. First here and then there
the mass of undignified humanity thrashed across the floor.
Some prodded at it ineffectively with their swords. Don
Cesar held himself aloof from a rough and tumble which
consorted ill with his Castilian dignity. Someone else saw
O'Neill's head emerge from the muddle and kicked it
shrewdly with a heavy boot. Others saw their opportunity
and, falling on their knees, struck with their knives, over
and over again.

And there, on the earthen floor of an inn, the Captain-
General of Leon – self-appointed – died. The military des-
potism he had set up was thus marked, in the best tradi-
tions of such a form of rule, by a palace revolution
initiated by the defection of the captain of the bodyguards.

It had taken much to kill an unarmed man. O'Neill's
body bore as many wounds as any Cæsar's, as he lay there
in a wide pool of blood in the semi-darkness. Only one
candle had survived the struggle, and this stood in its
candlestick with a long sooted wick protruding from its
flame, stinking abominably. El Platero snuffed it carefully,
and then relit the other candles from it. The other men
were recovering from the struggle, breathing hard. Volpe
was trying to adjust his tunic, which had been torn right
across the breast. Elizalde, gasping with pain, was sitting
in the blood on the floor nursing his shattered shoulder.
Don Cesar bent over the body sprawled upon the ground.

'He solved the problem for us,' said Don Cesar.

It was perhaps a more kindly epitaph than a dead des-
pot deserved.

CHAPTER XVI

As THOUGH the very elements wished to mark their approval of recent events, the next morning dawned bright and promising. The icy wind had dropped, the rain had ceased, and the sun broke early through the mist to warm the aching limbs of the marching soldiers, and to harden the miry roads, and to comfort the hearts of all. The army of Leon was on the march just as if its General had not died during the night. It continued to sprawl forward across the plains like some shapeless monster – an acephalous monster, now – like some vast amœboid organism trickling over the plains towards the great road from France to Madrid along which ran the life blood of the French army.

The many leaders had been wise to keep their several sections on the move. No one was likely to ask questions about a dead general in the course of a long and sultry march, or while recovering from it afterwards – and while the prospect still dangled before them of new conquests to be achieved. Not the stupidest man in the whole army could be unaware of the existence of that road, and of its supreme importance in the war; nor could he fail to thrill at the prospect of closing it to French supplies and messages.

Besides, there was little motive for asking questions. El Platero's men obeyed el Platero's orders, and Urquiola's men Urquiola's. No one was specially interested in O'Neill's continued existence. The men who had once formed O'Neill's band, and those who had once formed el Bilbanito's, had grown accustomed to their combined duties as headquarters guard and men of the artillery train, and in consequence to obedience to Jorge. Their experiences as guerilleros had taught them that too great an interest in the doings of their superiors was unhealthy. Some men had opened their eyes wide at sight of Jorge astride the big grey horse which O'Neill had ridden, but they knew better than to open their mouths as well. There had been no love for O'Neill.

As for Jorge, he was as happy as a king. The sun shone, and he had a good horse under him, and he was undisputed master of the gun. He had come to love that big eighteen-pounder. There seemed to be some fraternal bond between him and it. There was an odd physical resemblance, certainly. Although Jorge, at eighteen, had hardly come yet to his full strength, his figure was immense and square, with vast thews, and on foot there was a roll in his gait queerly like the gun's motion on a rocky road. He loved the gun for its deadly precision, for its crushing power. Its pig-headed obstinacy when being pulled over broken country was to Jorge's mind (which was also somewhat inclined to obstinacy) much more of a virtue than a vice.

As Jorge rode along beside the gun team he felt — even if he was not yet conscious of them — unwonted prickings of ambition within him. He hoped — he even nearly believed — that he was on the high road to eminence as a soldier. Certainly the council of war which had been held the night before over O'Neill's dead body included him in it as a matter of course. It was assumed without question that he was to be responsible for the artillery; as chief of a detachment he could rate himself on an equality with Don Cesar Urquiola, a gentleman of the bluest blood of Castile, or with Alvarez, the most famous of Mina's lieutenants. He could even look down upon the inexperienced country gentlemen who found themselves in command of the battalions of local levies. At a conservative estimate he was not lower than fifth or sixth in the unstated hierarchy of the army. With a little good fortune he might find himself soon in command of all the ten thousand men of the army of Leon, able to proclaim himself Captain-General if he wished, and with a long future of military glory before him. The prospect more than compensated him for the saddle soreness and stiffness which almost prevented him from walking at the end of the day.

These physical disabilities did not deter him at all from limping round among the men that evening. The mercurial temperament of the mountaineers had risen with the improvement in the weather; perhaps also with the unexplained disappearance of O'Neill; and the mountaineers' light spirits infected the graver men of the plains. The guitars of the south and the bagpipes of the north blended in a raucous discord as the men danced in their bivouacs and billets. There was laughter and merriment, and, perhaps because there was food in plenty in this halting place, perhaps because – as seems barely possible – Jorge's new-born pride communicated itself to the others, everyone was newly filled with confidence. On the next day's march the men roared out songs as they tramped along, and the drums rattled and roared with a gaiety they might almost have learned from the French, and Jorge rode along among them, shrinking from contact with the saddle, but rapt in blissful dreams of future triumphs and glory, as unwarrantable as they were ill-defined.

Now they came to the road at last. El Bilbanito had hardly dared to think of reaching the road. O'Neill, before his megalomania overmastered him, had thought of it as a very desirable but hardly attainable ideal. It was Jorge who had finally brought the gun there. It ran as straight as a bullet flies, as far as the eye could reach in either direction across the plain. Fifty miles to the north it had quitted the mountains of the Basque provinces, where Mina and Longa and el Marquesito threatened it; fifty miles to the south it charged the slopes of the Guadarrama, where el Empecinado lurked. For two years no Spanish force had ventured to approach it here, in the heart of Old Castile.

The great roadmakers of the world would not consider it to be a very remarkable road. It was narrow, it was not too durably paved; its gradients were not engineered with particular skill. But for all that, it was a very remarkable road for Spain; if only for the fact that it was the one beneficial public work undertaken during two centuries by the dynasty for which Spain was at that moment so lavishly pouring out her blood. It was the link which joined Spain to Europe; the stages along it, Vittoria, Burgos, Madrid and the rest marked the flow and the ebb of the Moorish conquest just as they were to mark later on the ebb and the flow of the French conquest. It was at once the main artery and the main nerve of the French army of occupation. Along it came the recruits, the stores, the money, and the information which enabled King Joseph to rule in Madrid, and Massena to confront Wellington in Portugal, and Soult to hold down the opulent south.

In the mountains to the north and south experience and necessity had taught the French to fortify almost every yard of its course; here in the plains there had been no need so far and small indication of any eventual necessity. But at this vital strategic point, where the road was joined by the by-road from Leon, and where it crossed the Salas River by a long stone bridge, Bessières had taken the precaution of building a fortress. Here convoys could rest in security, and here was a convenient depot wherein could be concentrated the tribute and the supplies wrung from the surrounding country.

It proved its value now; when the news had come that Leon had risen in revolt, that the garrisons had been massacred, and that a new Spanish army was pouring down towards the road, the little garrisons of Old Castile had gathered here for protection; the convoys bound south and the convoys bound north had halted here, and measures had been taken to offer a desperate defence while messengers had sped north and south with the alarm, to summon the inevitable armies of relief.

Jorge, filled with a most delicious sense of his own importance, trotted forward on the big grey horse, Urquiola and Alvarez at his side, to reconnoitre this new object of attack. The army stopped to rest, higgledy-piggledy along five miles of road, save for Urquiola's lancers, who were riding in groups over the plain. The fort did not look as formidable as La Merced, because it did not stand on such a dominating height, nor as the citadel of Leon, because it could be inspected from a much greater distance. Jorge could see long walls of grey stone, and storehouses within and a central citadel. At the foot of the walls might be a dry ditch, and in the bottom of the ditch might be palisades. Jorge rode forward to confirm these suspicions, Urquiola and Alvarez jingling beside him. There came a puff of smoke from the wall; a cannon ball pitched close to them in a cloud of dust and bounced onward over the plain.

'That was heavy metal,' said Alvarez, eyeing the length of the range.

Jorge said nothing. He was so interested in this business of reconnaissance that the fact that he was under fire made no impression on him. He rode on through the sparse corn. Another jet of smoke showed on the wall. This time the ball pitched almost in front of them and ricocheted past them.

'Garcia told us that they have eighteen-pounders mounted on the wall,' said Alvarez.

Jorge pressed on through the dust cloud which obscured his view. It was from this side he must make his attack; the other was guarded by the river. As far as he could see, apart from that, one starting point was as good as another on this naked plain. But there might be something, some fold in the ground, some dry watercourse, which might facilitate the attack.

A third shot from the fort screamed close over their heads; they felt the wind of its passage.

'Haven't you seen enough yet?' growled Alvarez anxiously. 'There's no sense in being shot at without an object.'

He quieted down his plunging horse and addressed himself to Jorge more directly than ever.

'Come back now,' he said. 'They'll hit us next round.'

Jorge shook his hand from his arm and rode diagonally forward still, his attention all concentrated in the unwonted stream of thoughts passing through his mind.

'Then go on if you want to,' said Alvarez. 'I shall not come; my men have still need of me. Shall we go back, Don Cesar?'

Urquiola turned his horse without another word, and the two trotted back. Jorge rode on. He approached the river bank on one side of the fort, wheeled the grey horse about and rode round the fort till he neared the river on the other side. They gave up firing eighteen-pounders at him as he came nearer, and opened instead with handier field guns. Several enthusiasts on the wall took their muskets and tried long shots with them; even at three hundred yards it was just possible to hit a man on a horse with a musket if one fired enough times. Bullets kicked up the dust round his horse's feet. They roused him from his abstraction in the end by wheeling an eighteen-pounder round again and firing at him with grape. It was long range for grape shot, but the aim was good. The bullets tore up the ground all round him; it seemed for a second as if the grey horse was wading knee-deep in a river of grape.

Jorge woke like a man from a dream. Miraculously he had not been hit, nor his horse. He shook his reins and cantered away, to where half the army had gathered to watch the performance.

'Well?' asked Alvarez, anxiety in his narrow eyes. 'Can

you take the place?'

Alvarez and Urquiola had decided that they neither of them liked the look of the fortress of Salas at all, and they were anxious to thrust the responsibility of a decision upon Jorge's shoulders.

'Of course I can,' said Jorge. It never occurred to him that his marvellous eighteen-pounder could fail.

'Then get to work,' said Alvarez. 'I will take my men northward up the road to cover you.'

Alvarez had by no means sufficient trust in the eighteen-pounder – or at least in Jorge's management of it – to risk his men's lives and his own reputation in the attempt.

Jorge found himself there on the road, just out of range of the big guns, with the siege of a powerful second-class fortress on his hands. He had never even seen a real fortress before. But the other commanding officers gathered round him for orders with pathetic confidence. They looked upon him – as Alvarez and Urquiola did not – as O'Neill's successor. They were quick to toady to him, quick to defer to authority, or quick to evade the responsibility which Jorge assumed without a thought.

Jorge peered down the road under his hand. He was under the necessity of working out for himself the highly technical art of siegecraft from first principles. 'Parallels' and 'approaches' meant nothing to him at all, but he knew that no troops could advance against that fortress over that naked plain under the fire which would be turned on them. But he had heard of trenches – he had even seen one or two minor trenches dug during the sieges O'Neill had conducted. By a trench the men could approach the fort; but naturally the trench must not point directly at it, or the artillery would play straight down it. The trench must point towards some point just outside the fortress, and then at a convenient distance must change direction and point towards the opposite side, and so on, approaching the fort in zigzags. Then, when the trench was close to the fort, the big gun must break the walls, and the infantry rise up out of the trench and storm the breach. A very technical art seems simple when stated in simple terms.

Jorge, privately inspired, rose to greater heights still. If the trenches were to be begun out of cannon range – a mile and a half from the fort, say – and carried forward in zigzags by work at one end only, it would be months before the approaches neared the walls. But Jorge had not been a guerillero all these years for nothing. He had acquired an eye for ground. There were two successive, almost imperceptible undulations in the plain; the crest of either would shelter men from fire. The nearer one was no more than half a mile from the walls. If the trench were to begin there on a long front much time and trouble would be saved. True, men coming to and going from it would be under fire, but what was night for if not to conceal besiegers? And when circumstances permitted they might dig a communication trench for use in daylight.

The first trench would have to be dug at night, too, and Jorge had had a fair experience of military operations at night – trust a guerillero for that. He knew how incredibly easy it was for them to go wrong in the darkness, and he was keenly appreciative of the necessity of making every possible preparation beforehand. If the trench was to be dug at night it must be planned and marked in the daytime. Jorge abruptly issued orders for the cutting of a number of pointed stakes, and for strips of white cloth to be tied to them. As night fell, in the last feeble glimmering of daylight, he went out himself to the second fold in the ground and drove those stakes in a long line beneath the tiny crest of the insignificant ridge.

CHAPTER XVII

A TALENTED engineer officer, set to besiege the fortress of Salas, would have acted just like Jorge. The only difference would have been that the engineer would have had a vocabulary with which to describe his actions. On the first night of the siege, his report would have stated, he would have 'broken ground' and 'thrown up his first parallel' in 'dead ground' half a mile from the fortress. But, just like Jorge, he would have sent forward a 'covering party' in skirmishing order to guard against a sortie, and, having lined up his 'working party' along the stakes previously driven in, he would have bade them dig like devils, throwing the earth forward in a 'parapet' along the very line which Jorge's untutored eye had selected as most suitable.

Perhaps because Jorge's methods were so strictly orthodox the besieged discovered his nocturnal activities at once. They fired a few cannon balls at his workmen, but, not being sure of their aim in the dark, they took to a much more effective weapon. There were four big howitzers within the place, and with these they began dropping shells just over the line of the ridge, whose range was naturally known to them to a yard. They did a good deal of damage. They blew down parapets, they killed workmen half a dozen at a time.

But Jorge's men stuck to it. Some of them were miners, and most of the rest of them had been tillers of the soil until recently. They were accustomed and hardened to digging; more important still, they had never so far besieged a place without taking it. They, in their ignorance, were far from sharing the doubts of Alvarez or Urquiola. They dug with enthusiasm. They dragged their dead comrades out of the way and went on digging. It was not long before the howitzers lost the range so that the shells only rarely interfered with the work. By dawn there was a long narrow seam of trench all along the fold of the ground, and six hundred men were comfortably settled into it. They were in a state of siege as long as daylight lasted as much as the garrison of the fortress was, because the artillery fire cut them off from supplies from the rear, but they did not mind that today. They rested content, and began to reduce the trench to that happy state of filth which made things home-like, while two small working parties began the one to push a communication trench slowly to the rear and the other to sap forward towards the fortress from one flank of the trench.

On this advancing trench the garrison turned all their guns, big guns, field guns, and howitzers. They knocked down big sections of the parapet, and killed a good many of the working party. Even Jorge saw that what the besiegers ought to do was to build a battery somewhere along the line of their 'first parallel,' arm it with big guns, and so keep down the fire of the fortress. But Jorge had only one eighteen-pounder, and he was not going to risk it in a duel so unequal; he had to reserve it for breaching the wall when the approaches were completed. Perhaps when the field guns struggled up from the rear he might use those, although they would be too small to do much damage. Meanwhile men's lives must be sacrificed in the absence of artillery. The murderous work at the sap-head proceeded steadily. The sturdy miners dug furiously despite their losses.

Partly their enthusiasm was kindled by Jorge's example. He worked as hard as any; he seemed to be quite indifferent to danger. As a matter of fact, he actually was indifferent. He was so intensely interested in this new enterprise that he quite forgot about the danger he was running. It was something new to him to hold this high command, to bear this great responsibility. It was peculiarly gratifying to see his siege works growing under his eyes. It satisfied his creative impulses.

But while he was so engrossed in the bustle and toil at the sap-head he was suddenly interrupted by a messenger who came pushing his way down the trench to him. The other officers urgently requested his attendance at headquarters. Jorge cursed aloud, but comically, somehow, so that the men digging beside him laughed. With a parting incitement to work harder still he left them, and they cheered him as he went — so much had his popularity grown overnight.

Jorge made his way along the trench, scrambled out over the back, and ran the gauntlet of the enemy's fire as he hastened across the open country. But nobody bothered to fire guns at a single man on foot. At the roadside were Urquiola and Alvarez and Delgado, with half a dozen of Urquiola's lancers; and a man in peasant's clothes was sitting on the ground, his face grey with fatigue. Behind him his small horse, grey with dust, hung his head in exhaustion. Urquiola handed Jorge the note the man had brought, and Jorge looked at it upside down and handed it back.

'What does it say?' asked Jorge, who naturally could not read.

'It is from Brother Bernard,' said Urquiola, 'the man who put the arsenic in the flour at Leon.'

'I am glad to hear from him again,' said Jorge. It was wonderful how his new activity was bringing him out of his previous dumbness.

'There is a regiment of the French Guard marching down from Biscay, he says,' said Urquiola. 'He is out with all the peasants he can raise — which are not very many.'

'Nor likely to be,' said Jorge. O'Neill had swept every man he could catch into the ranks of this army now gathered before Salas. 'And how many Frenchmen did you say?'

'A regiment,' said Urquiola, testily.

Jorge, groping in his mind, was just able to recapture his recollection of what a regiment was – two or three battalions; altogether from one to two thousand men.

'Of the Guard,' added Alvarez, sombrely.

'Yes,' said Jorge, 'I expect Brother Bernard finds his hands full.'

Jorge in his guerillero days had come up against the Guard once or twice, and he knew what kind of soldiers they were.

'Brother Bernard says that there is no stopping them. They march where they will. He asks for help. He asks us for cannons.'

'Cannons?' said Jorge. In his mind's eye he saw the army's field guns embogged and deserted, left without teams fifty miles away. It would be a week before they came up.

'It must be guns,' said Alvarez. 'What can we do against a regiment of the Guard here on this cursed plain?'

Alvarez could never mention the plains without bitterness. He had learned his soldier's trade under Mina in the mountains of Navarre. But Jorge, just as well as Alvarez, could picture the attempt to engage the Guard on the plains. No Spanish troops, however numerous, could face them. They would shatter any infantry force opposing them; they would beat off any cavalry. They might march unchecked even into Salas, and the addition of their strength to that of the garrison would render a siege impossible; it would in fact imperil the whole army.

'How far are they off now?' asked Jorge.

'They were thirty miles away at dawn this morning, when this man left Brother Bernard,' said Urquiola.

'Thirty miles? Then they may be here at nightfall. And we must meet them as far from here as we can.'

'We know that,' snapped Alvarez. 'Can you move your gun at once?'

'Yes.'

'Then for God's sake come now. Don Cesar, are your men ready?'

'Bring my horse!' shouted Jorge to his orderly. Within three days it had grown to be perfectly natural to Jorge to call to a man to bring his horse. The thrill of pleasure which the giving of the order had originally caused him, already growing stale, was quite unnoticed now in the excitement of the moment.

The evils of a divided command were not at all apparent at this crisis. The situation was too simple, the need was too urgent, everyone was too enthusiastic in the cause for opinion to be divided or for irresolution to display itself. Soon, drawn by thirty mules, yoked two by two, the big gun was off up the great paved road. On this admirable surface, and under the goadings of the excited muleteers, the mules made prodigious speed. At quite three miles an hour the big gun was dragged along; it crashed and rattled over the inequalities of the *pavé*, rolling about like a ship at sea. After it came thirty mules of the pack train, plodding stolidly along under their vast burdens of cannon balls and powder – some of them (those with careful drivers) bearing a net of forage as well.

Don Cesar's lancers were already clattering up the road far ahead, and hot on their tracks marched Alvarez' Navarrese. The garrison of the fort saw them go, but it was only a detachment after all. There were still several thousand men in loose formation round the place. A sally at present would be objectless and dangerous.

CHAPTER XVIII

THE FOURTH Regiment of the Fusiliers of the Imperial Guard – the premier regiment of what was colloquially termed the Young Guard – had had a disturbing march. They had been sent over the mountains from Biscay in consequence of the wild rumours which had drifted into that province regarding the situation in Leon. Even the men in the ranks had heard the fantastic stories; they had heard whispers of universal revolt, of huge Spanish armies, miraculously sprung from the ground, of fortresses taken, and even unbelievable tales of the poisoning of the whole garrison of the citadel of Leon.

The fact that no messengers came in from Leon did not do much towards confirming these rumours. The French garrison of every Spanish province was accustomed to being quite isolated from every other province for weeks at a time, thanks to the activities of the guerilleros who lurked in the mountains. It was a usual assumption that no message was safe unless four hundred men at least escorted it. But the rumours had grown insistent, and at last the Military Governor of Biscay had felt compelled to act upon them. Only by pinching and scraping, and by careful redistribution of his garrisons, had he been able to set free a single regiment and launch it over the passes with orders to get into touch at all costs with the troops guarding the main line of communications. Wellington was loose in the south, he knew, and the knowledge was enough to make any French general nervous; moreover, when every available man had already been drawn off to oppose him there was always this difficulty about finding a sufficient force to reopen communications.

The march of the Fusiliers had all the nightmare

quality which characterized the march of small bodies of French troops in Spain. There had been the usual sniping from hillsides, and the usual number of sentries found in the morning with their throats cut. They marched along roads without a soul being seen; they entered villages without a single inhabitant – everything was left deserted at their approach. The hard-bitten veterans of the Guard took care in every village to see that nothing of value was left behind when they quitted the place, although the loot was poor because every village had been plundered half a dozen times already. It usually happened from carelessness or malice that the villages were set on fire as they marched out.

Down in the plains the conditions seemed more ominous than ever. The number of irregulars hanging round their flanks as they marched apparently increased. They could see gangs of fifty or so marching parallel to them, ready to run at the first attack, but equally ready to cut a straggler's throat or to cut off a small body of marauders, and much too fleet of foot for the heavily laden infantry men to catch them. The march seemed to the men in the ranks like the passage of a swimmer in the sea. No individual droplet of water could offer him any measurable resistance; but the water would close behind him as readily as he cleft it in front, and if he tried to swim too far the water would overpower him in the end.

Then they reached Saldaña, and they knew matters were serious, for where the tricolour had once waved they now saw the red and gold of Spain, and where they had anticipated welcome they now received musket shots and yells of defiance from the fanatics who had shut themselves up in the place. There was no retaking the place; as the Spaniards had discovered long before, these little fortresses were impregnable to infantry without artillery. The Fusiliers swerved aside and marched to Santa Eulalia, and Santa Eulalia was in the hands of Spaniards, too. Surely

Leon, the capital, with its garrison of a thousand men and its formidable commandant would still be holding out? But when they marched up the road to Leon they found the gates shut against them, and the walls manned by excited mobs who fired off muskets at them at impossible range but who could still be relied upon to beat off any attack unsupported by big guns. That impression as if a sea was closing about them was intensified. Already the sea had engulfed many of the refuges where they had hoped to rest awhile.

On their march back to Carrion they met the first real opposition in the field. A few score misguided peasants tried to hold the crossing where the road passed one of the ravines which seam the plain. But it had been folly to suppose that a mere ravine and a few brave men could stop two battalions of the Guard. The Fusiliers rejoiced at the prospect of action. In front one battalion threatened the crossing. Half a mile away the other battalion swarmed down the side of the ravine, fought their way waist deep across the raging water, up the other side, and came down on the flank of the opposition almost before the poor fools realized that their flank might be turned. Some they caught and bayoneted, and the rest ran like hares across the plain – half a squadron of dragoons would have cut them all to pieces, but with Wellington loose in the south there was not even half a squadron of dragoons to spare in the north.

It was only by the greatest exertions that the officers could prevail on the maddened soldiers to spare two or three of the men they caught. It was of the utmost importance that information should be gathered, and it was only from prisoners that information could be got. The prisoners did not tell willingly, but they talked after a time, after 'the question' had been applied to them – a most significant expression. Kept rigidly apart, and questioned by men who had learned how to extract information from recalcitrant Spaniards, and then requestioned on points in which their tales differed, they told all they knew.

Pieced together as far as might be – for the wretched men had only fragmentary knowledge themselves – the story they told was like some fantastic romance of the old chivalry in which the supernatural was inextricably blended with the truth. They told of a marvellous man called O'Neill, who had marched down from the mountains with a great army, and with a new sort of gun which had blown in the gates of the city of Leon from five miles away. He had ranged the length and breadth of Leon, killing all who had offered him opposition, Spaniards and Frenchmen alike. The peasant's hearsay account of the executions in the Plaza Mayor took on the aspect of the multiple human sacrifices of a King of Dahomey. They knew something of the killing of the garrison of La Merced, and a little of the more prolonged, processional massacres of the garrisons which had capitulated and had been marched to the rear. Along with all this, and recurring like a refrain in their account of slaughter and destruction, they kept referring to someone else, vaguely identified as Brother Bernard, who apparently achieved by magic and prayer what was necessary to complete the work which O'Neill's strength had begun. It was from what they told that the Fusiliers were able to guess, with sickening hearts, at the poisoning of the garrison of Leon. And the peasants agreed that it was on account of orders issued by Brother Bernard that the peasantry were out in opposition to the Fusiliers. He had passed over the country with magic speed, and where he passed the men took arms and stood to fight the French. Finally, as to O'Neill, he had gone on with a great army, a very great army indeed, an enormous army – so said the peasants, whose eye had not been trained to appreciate the difference between a force of ten thousand men and one of a hundred thousand. He was gone to Madrid to hang King Joseph, and he would take King Ferdinand out of his dungeon and set him on the throne again.

Colonel Baron Laferrière, listening to all this muddle of fact and fiction, had to decide what to make of it. He had to discount some proportion of the obvious exaggeration about the size of O'Neill's army; he had to guess where its next blow might be struck; he had to make up his mind as to what was his duty to do next. Not without reason he was convinced that his men could march through any mass of hastily raised Spanish levies. He made up his mind that the best thing he could do would be to march by cross roads over the plain to the great road. There he would at least be at the place where his troops would do most good; he would complete the circle and march back to Biscay if he were wanted there, and, most important of all, he would carry the news of the rising and some facts about it to Burgos on his way.

After a few months of warfare in Spain every French officer learnt how necessary it was to take every opportunity to carry news – news in those isolated provinces where guerilleros haunted every road was the most precious military requirement that existed; the march of every column had to be modified so that it could escort despatches as well as carry out whatever other function was allotted it.

So the Fusiliers of the Guard turned eastward, and marched along the country tracks over the plains. They were a very fine spectacle, in their smart blue tunics and their white breeches and black gaiters. The stream of tall black bearskins ornamented each with a long, gaudy red feather poured along the rough tracks; in the centre of the column between the two battalions the band blared away nobly, and the drums thundered and rolled, and overhead on its long staff the silver regimental eagle flashed as it caught the sun. These were the men who had marched into every capital in Europe, the men who had decided the fate of Europe at Wagram. Colonel Baron Laferrière was the man who had headed the charge at Jena which brought down in ruins the greatest military monarchy of the world.

It was ironical that they should now be ringed in by armed peasants. The men of whom the kings of the world went in terror were glad to halt for the night in mudbuilt villages, where they made their meagre supper of corn looted from the barns, pounded between stones, and toasted into tasteless girdle cakes. And a knife between the ribs killed a sentry of the Guards just as surely as it would the youngest conscript in the Imperial army.

They were thirteen hundred strong, and the men who scrambled through the fields beside them, who took long shots at intervals into the column, who pestered and worried them so remorselessly, were perhaps less than two hundred. If there had been ten times as many they would have effected no more, and perhaps their numbers would have tempted them to attempt more and fail; but that was cold comfort to Colonel Baron Laferrière when he saw his big sunburnt men, veterans of Marengo and Austerlitz, tumble over when the muskets squibbed off in a distant ditch.

It was near evening at the end of one of these nightmare days when they reached the great road at last. Southward it went like a bullet across the dreary plain towards Madrid; northward it plunged into the mountains, blue in the distant horizon, where lay Burgos, and their friends, and a meat ration, and a rest from this continual sniping. While the men were cooking their evening meal – tearing out doors and window frames for fuel – Colonel Baron Laferrière thought he heard a significant sound to the southward. It was gunfire, he thought, and a man who had heard artillery firing on fifty battlefields over Europe could not be mistaken. But when he called the other officers' attention to it they could hear nothing, nor could the sergeant-major when he was consulted. Even the colonel could hear nothing again now. He felt he must have been mistaken, although he could not really believe it. Truly he could hear nothing now. Jorge had by now turned his horse away from the fortress of Salas and the garrison had ceased trying to hit with grape the fool on the grey horse who had ridden so close up to their walls.

Yet in the night the adjutant came and woke the colonel where he lay wrapped in his cloak in the flea-ridden inn. Out in the courtyard several officers and men were listening intently. As the colonel joined them he was quite certain that he heard the distant thud-thud of guns. A chorus of exclamations from the listeners confirmed him in his belief. The sergeant-major lifted his head from the drum on which he had laid it and announced positively that there was firing somewhere to the south. Everyone listened again. In the still night the sound came to them clearly enough – the garrison of Salas was firing at the first parallel which was being thrown up under Jorge's direction.

Colonel Baron Laferrière had no difficulty next morning in deciding what he ought to do. Thirty miles down the road was the fortress of Salas, one of the most important posts on all the Royal Road. The gunfire – men still affirmed that they heard it, despite the bustle of the regiment's getting under arms – showed that Salas was beleaguered, presumably by the Leonese rabble which this unknown O'Neill had organized. Salas, Laferrière knew, was well provisioned – many were the convoys he had helped to escort thither – and with an adequate garrison ought to hold out indefinitely. Yet he could not be sure that the garrison was adequate. It was of the first importance that he should march there to reinforce it, breaking through the mob of besiegers. Then Salas would be safe until a real relieving force came up from the south.

The orders that Colonel Baron Laferrière gave on parade that morning turned the head of the column down the road towards Salas, instead of up it towards Burgos. It was then that Brother Bernard sent off his only horseman with the news to the Leonese army, while he himself mounted on his little white mule – his feet almost touched the ground on either side – to stimulate his peasantry into delaying the march of the French. Brother Bernard was quite as well aware of the importance of Salas as was Colonel Baron Laferrière.

The Fusiliers of the Guard marched southward down the great road. Still the pestilent irregulars pursued them. They acted more recklessly than usual, all the same. Several of them stayed firing until too late from the ditches and dry watercourses in which they had hidden themselves, and were caught by the advanced guard and killed. All through the morning the Fusiliers saw in full view the leader of these pests – a monk in greyish brown robe astride a white mule. Once he approached so close that the colonel departed from his rigid rule of paying no attention to irregulars, and, halting the column, had the leading platoon fire a volley at him. But he trotted off quite unharmed through the gust of bullets; it was a waste of five minutes and fifty rounds.

Then, as the weary morning wore on, and the heat of the sun grew more crushing, a new enemy appeared. A long column of horsemen came trotting up the road towards them, and, as they grew near, they spread out over the plain in little squadrons, ringing in the marching column from a safe distance. The colonel cared nothing for them; they were no danger, but merely an additional nuisance. There were no Spanish cavalry in existence which could charge five hundred men together, and these poor levies, on their Lilliputian horses, could do his regiment no harm as long as it kept closed and ready to form square in the event of a rush. But they were undoubtedly a nuisance. The Fusiliers had to abandon their comfortable marching order in column of sixes and form quarter column of companies astride the road, slowing their rate of march and worrying the men with the need for careful dressing and distancing. And the endangered flank guards and advanced guard had to be called in, so that the irregulars on foot could creep in close to the column and fire into the vulnerable masses.

CHAPTER XIX

JORGE LEFT the gun and the ammuniton train making its slow way up the road, and, digging his heels into the grey horse's sides, galloped on ahead whither Urquiola and Alvarez had vanished over the grey-green plain. Thoughts and ideas were pouring through his mind like a millstream. He knew nothing of textbook principles of war; he had never heard of 'the intelligent combination of the three arms' or any of the other ideals held up before aspiring generals. But he knew that ahead of him was an enemy whom the cavalry could not break, whom the infantry could not face, but who would be quite helpless before a skilful employment of the big gun which he so dearly loved. So engrossed was he with the plan of action which he was evolving in his slow brain that he never noticed the agony which riding caused his skinned and blistered body.

He was looking for a safe ambush for the gun – a place from which he could open fire unexpectedly and at close range, and yet have time to fire a dozen rounds without having to fight for his life. As he urged the big grey horse up the road his eyes swept the plain to left and to right in search of the sort of place he had in mind. He found it a couple of miles higher up.

Here a steep banked ravine seamed the plain, crossing the road at an acute angle. It was not in the least impassable to infantry, but it would be an awkward obstacle, causing delay and disorder. The massive stone bridge by which the road crossed it was far too solid a structure for him to think of destroying it in the hour which was all he had to spare; but the destruction of the bridge was not essential to his plan. For on the near side of the ravine, where it flanked the road beyond the bridge, stood a solitary cottage, of the usual sun-dried brick, with beside it some sort of cow-house of the same material.

Jorge urged the big horse through the crops towards the cottage, clattering up to the door. There were two young women working in the field near at hand who looked up, and an old bent woman came out through the door at the sound of his approach, with two small children clinging to her skirts. Jorge gave them neither word nor look – possibly he did not even see them – and the children looked at him wondering as he wheeled the big grey horse here and there, riding round the cowshed and the dung heap, taking in the details of the position before he turned his horse's head back to the road and rode like the wind to set his plan in motion.

Alvarez, wondering how he could use his Navarrese infantry with their untrustworthy leaven of Leonese levies in this featureless plain against this solid mass of disciplined troops heard the hoofbeats of the grey horse as it came up to him at frantic speed. Jorge reined the sweating animal up beside him; his eyes blazed strangely out of his face caked with dust and sweat. He poured out his plan. Excitement lent him unwonted eloquence. Even Alvarez the sceptical and cautious took fire. It was at least a plan, while Alvarez had none to offer. Within five minutes four hundred of Alvarez' men were marching back down the road again as fast as they could set foot to the ground, under the burning sun, to the bridge they had crossed an hour before.

Jorge gave no thought to the scene before him. He did

not spare the Fusiliers of the Guard the grace of a glance. The visual imagination which excitement and action had roused in him had pictured the whole scene before he set eyes on it – the long beautiful lines of bearskins and plumes moving regularly across the plain, the eagle flashing overhead, the bayonets gleaming through the dust; and the knots of horsemen prowling round out of range, helpless and disconsolate.

He found Urquiola riding with a hundred of his Castilians, grimy pennons fluttering from the lance points. Two years before Urquiola would have charged them, to red ruin and certain death, but in two years of war Urquiola had learned that it was folly to charge on these weakly horses against unshaken infantry. But it was a bitter pill to swallow, to follow these French like jackals, picking up the stragglers who fell out with sunstroke, and apart from that acting more like an escort of honour than like an enemy as they made their triumphant way to Salas.

To Urquiola Jorge poured out his plan again. With a sweep of his arm he pointed out the features of the land – it was strange how quickly Jorge had acquired the general's eye for country – and next minute another detachment of lancers was trotting off along the route Jorge had pointed out, turning the end of the ravine so as to be on the further side before the French could reach it. Then Jorge galloped back down the road again to where the gun was lumbering up towards him; he was wild with panic lest he had not time to get all things ordered before the French should reach the ravine.

The children at the cottage had not yet ceased from asking questions about the man on the big grey horse who had galloped up and galloped away again – questions which their grandmother could not answer – when things began to happen which ended their questions. A long double line of mules came tugging and straining over the field to the cottage, drawing after them an immense cannon. The sweating men who goaded the mules said something to their grandmother which set the poor old lady into a terrible panic. Their mother and their aunt came running in from the field, and began despairingly to bundle together pots and pans and the treasures of the household, but when the man on the grey horse came up they had to leave off doing this and hurry out of the cottage with the children, aimlessly out across the fields. The children whimpered, and struggled vainly as they were dragged away. They wanted to stay and see what was going to happen, and to hear the big cannon fired; already, with shouts and gaspings for breath, it had been hauled through the yard and wheeled round beside the cottage wall so that its long grim muzzle pointed out round the corner. There were other men, too, who came clattering into the cottage, and broke holes in the walls, and who loaded their guns with long ram-rods, and who turned the precious goats loose, and who yet had time and thought to spare to wring the chickens' necks and hang the bodies to their belts.

Jorge had found time for everything. The gun was well concealed between the cottage and the dung heap. The cottage was garrisoned; the banks of the ravine were lined with skirmishers. Urquiola and his lancers were waiting ready in line two hundred yards away. Jorge loaded the gun with care. He was meticulous about the ladleful of gunpowder which was scooped into the gun muzzle and rammed carefully down. He saw that the touch-hole was filled with loose powder. He rammed down with his own hands one of the long cylindrical tin boxes filled with musket balls which constituted the projectile known as 'canister' – Jorge had never seen canister used in action before. Close beside the gun stood a further dozen rounds of canister, a dozen of grape, a dozen of roundshot. A ladleful of powder was ready for instant reloading. There were two slow-matches ready burning – Spanish slow-match was unreliable material with a distressing habit of going out at a crucial moment. The mules had all been sent half a mile away so that in the event of disaster they would not be captured, and the French would have no means of dragging away the big gun. For the last time Jorge looked along the sights of the gun and saw that it bore exactly on the point of the road nearest the cottage.

The Fourth Regiment of the Fusiliers of the Guard came marching steadily over the plain. The afternoon was well advanced now, and they had been marching since dawn under a burning sun. They had eaten nothing since morning, and all they had drunk had been the contents of their water bottles. One or two men had collapsed under the strain. One or two men had been killed by long shots. One or two wounded were being carried on the officers' horses – no wounded could possibly be abandoned to the mercy of Spanish irregulars.

But the honour of the Imperial Guard was involved. At the thought of that the big, sunburnt, moustached soldiers pulled themselves erect again under their heavy burdens, as a child will wipe his eyes when told that no really big boy ever cries. Their officers told them that their troubles were nearly over, that Salas lay only six miles ahead, and that in Salas they would find rest, and security, and food, and a bottle of wine for every man. They marched on hopefully.

At the sight of the ravine, and the bridge, and the cottage, with the enemy drawing in closely at this point, Colonel Laferrière realized that it was here that the enemy had decided to make his decisive stand; and the colonel's heart grew proportionately lighter. The ravine was not the sort of obstacle which would stop his hard-bitten men. They would shatter the enemy's line at the bridge, and with any sort of good fortune they would deal the enemy such a blow that they would not be molested again that day. He would have to guard his rear while attacking in front, and it might be better to give his men ten minutes' rest before sending them forward, but his troubles were over, he thought. At his word the long lines of plumes stood fast, and the men wiped their sweating faces, and saw to the priming of their muskets, and looked forward expectantly to taking their revenge on the Spaniards.

Then the drums rolled, wilder and wilder in the *pas de charge*. The officers moved out to the front, with their swords flashing in the sun. The long lines came forward like walls. The company of voltigeurs ran out ahead, the green plumes waving gallantly, to the edge of the ravine, and the solid lines followed them. Jorge squinted along the sights of the gun. He blew the smouldering slow-match into a brisker glow, and pressed it into the touch-hole.

An eighteen-pounder round of canister contained four hundred musket balls. The thin tin box which held them served to lessen their spread just a little, like the choke bore of a shot gun. Four hundred bullets were flung at once with precision into the flank of the advancing lines. No infantry battalion – not even an English one – could have fired a volley of such deadliness .The Guard staggered with the shock.

The gunners tried to peer through the billowing smoke to see the effect of the shot, and those who could see raised a cheer at the destruction it had caused, but Jorge, cursing at the top of his voice, recalled them to their duty. Already he had wiped out the gun. He ladled the powder into the muzzle, and forced it down with the rammer and the wad. He swung a new canister into the gun and rammed that. He flung his weight upon the breech as if by his own unaided exertions he would run the gun up into position again. They helped him wildly. The muzzle of the gun peered forward round the corner of the cottage again. Jorge looked along the sights, turned the lateral adjusting screw half a turn, looked again, and then grabbing a handful of powder, scattered it over the touch-hole. He caught up the slow-match and fired the gun. It roared out deafeningly, with the smoke pouring over them all. One born fool had forgotten to get out of the way of the recoil and lay shrieking with his leg under the wheel, but no one minded about that. Their business was to load and fire the gun as fast as it could be done.

The massed Fusiliers reeled as though every single man had been hit. Jorge had made 'intelligent use' not merely of the 'three arms' but of the general's fourth great weapon, surprise. No one had anticipated that blast of gunfire from the edge of that cottage. Not for the last year had the French in northern Spain encountered artillery in Spanish hands in the field. An eighteen-pounder firing canister can tear fearful gaps in massed infantry; and canister fired in from behind a flank when an attack is about to be made to the front is the most staggering of all.

There were a few young soldiers among the Guard; they tried to edge away from the merciless fire. The stoutest hearts – and the thickest heads – were bent on pursuing the attack, and pressing forward to the ravine across which the voltigeurs were already exchanging shots with the Spaniards. The more intelligent and less disciplined tried to alter the direction of the attack so as to rush the gun which was doing the damage. Into this wavering confusion came the fourth discharge to complete it. The colonel fell dead from his horse. The eagle fell in a wide arc as the standard bearer collapsed riddled with bullets. Someone else – one of the men who can be found to display Quixotic gallantry in any regiment – raised it up again.

But the mischief was done. After lurching in indecision the Guard began to move slowly away, along the ravine, away from the gun. No one directed the movement, no one ordered it, but all followed it. The old formation had disappeared. There were no more rigid lines. Even the two battalions were hopelessly intermingled. It was only a vast mob which stumbled over the plain.

The Spaniards yelled with triumph. They closed round

the shattered regiment like jackals round a wounded lion, firing at close range into the clumsy mass.

Jorge eyed the lengthening distance between his gun and the target and called for grapeshot. An eighteen-pound round of grape contains only thirty balls, each a little more than half a pound each, but thirty balls, each claiming its two or three victims, can smash a hole in a mass of human bodies. Jorge felt the inspiration of warfare boiling up inside him more furiously even than before. He called to his gun's crew to go on firing, rushed round the cottage to where the grey horse was tethered, and hauled himself into the saddle. Next moment he was galloping to the ravine. The good horse steadied himself at the obstacle and then leaped it like a stag. Jorge lost stirrups and reins and all, but he grabbed the saddle, regained his seat by a miracle and came flying up to where fifty of Urquiola's lancers were trotting cautiously after the French. Jorge shrieked 'Come on!' to them as he tore by, and they followed him. The lances came down to the horizontal, the sound of the hoof-beats rose to a roar through which the sound of the wind in the lance pennons could be distinctly heard.

A fresh blast of grape crashed into the mass of men and Jorge rode for the gap. Some of the Frenchmen – men who had beaten off the charge of the Russian Imperial cavalry at Austerlitz – faced about and raised their muskets, but it was only a few spattering shots which met the charge. The grey horse, badly wounded, rose on its hind legs and then came down among the Fusiliers kicking and struggling. Jorge, dazed, stupefied, without even a weapon, rolled in among them. But the lancers with that example before them charged home for the first time in their lives. The very pennons were soaked in the blood of Frenchmen. The impact of fifty galloping horses clove the mob in two parts, and each part disintegrated into smaller parts, into little groups that surrendered, into little groups that closed back to back and fought to the last, into isolated men stricken with panic who tried to run away over the plain through the victory-maddened Spaniards.

It was a pitiful sight to see the fine tall guardsmen in all the glory of bearskins and scarlet plumes and manly moustaches asking for their lives from the tatterdemalion semi-savages who seized them, but it was just as pitiful to see the others who scorned to ask for mercy being shot down one by one by the prowling guerilleros who would not close.

CHAPTER XX

THE GUN had won another victory. Previously it had only beaten down walls; but now it had beaten down discipline, organization, esprit de corps. It was a most resounding achievement. A whole regiment of the Imperial Guard had been destroyed. There would be a gap in the next army list to be issued in Paris. In the Almanac Imperial the name of Colonel Laferrière would have to be erased from the list of wearers of the Grand Cross of the Legion of Honour – his star was now borne upon the breast of a woman of the fields, who had received it from her lover who told a great tale of how he had won it in single combat hand to hand with the colonel himself. The eagle itself was in the hands of the victors, and was borne in triumph at the head of Alvarez' men when they marched back to Salas.

Despite all this Jorge did not seem to be spoilt by success. He was the same grinning giant, cracking the same jokes with the men who cheered him as the author of their triumph. For Jorge, although he might yearn for military distinction, could not visualize himself as a great man and had no touchy sense of his own dignity. When some enthusiast offered him a captured horse – most valuable personal plunder – to replace the dead grey he was actually embarrassed by the magnitude of the gift, but fortunately he remembered he had in his pocket the purse which he had taken from O'Neill's body, and he filled the man's hands with gold; he had never seen gold, save in the Cathedral of Santiago, until the war began, and he was conscious of a feeling of strangeness as he made the gesture. He shook off the awkwardness by a couple of jokes about those parts of his body which had no skin left on them, as he climbed up into the saddle.

It was only ten hours since he had set the gun in motion up the road from Salas, but it seemed like a week. The fields were littered with dead men, and there were heaps of wounded to mark the place where the blasts of canister had reached their mark. Some of them were still able to call for help; they had been thirsty before they had been wounded, and only God knew how they felt now. But they would not be thirsty long. The irregulars were going over the plain systematically, stripping the bodies, emptying pockets, and bringing rest to the wounded. Brother Bernard was among them. He took his spiritual duties seriously. As far as Latin and the wounded men's Spanish would permit, he confessed the wounded, and performed all the necessary offices before he cut their throats.

No one saw anything odd about that; irreligion had never been fashionable in Spain, and it was important to have souls, while as Brother Bernard's followers had never heard that there were such things as customs and usages of war they assumed that it was purely a matter of taste whether a helpless enemy's life should be spared or not. That Brother Bernard should cut a man's throat – in warfare, of course, not in civil life – meant no more and no less to their opinion of him than that he should wring a chicken's neck.

And Jorge was only eighteen, and he had been fighting since he was sixteen. Death was a commonplace to him, and he did not set the value on life which old age does. It did not move him in the least to pity to think of all those splendid men dead by his own act, and the huddled mass of prisoners doomed to a lingering death on the long march back to Leon and the mountains. He was merely elated at his own success, and he was still more pleased when he found that the whole force – Alvarez and Urquiola included – were awaiting his decision as to what should be done next. He had no hesitation in deciding to move back at once to continue the siege.

Alvarez and Urquiola had enough consideration for their own dignity not to come and ask for orders; but when Jorge gave the word for the gun to be got back on the road for Salas they went off hastily to their own contingents and issued similar orders. They knew that their men knew who had won the victory, and, at least until the glamour wore off, they knew that it would be as well to conform to his movements.

The victors rejoined the besiegers of Salas before the one survivor of the vanquished joined the besieged. Lieutenant Aubard, assistant adjutant of the Fourth Fusiliers of the Guard, had not meant to desert his regiment. He had wanted to die with them, although it was dreadful to die in such a fashion in an obscure skirmish in Spain with the Emperor eight hundred miles away. There had indeed been occasions when young Aubard had imagined himself being killed in action, but it had always involved a charge under the Emperor's own eye, on a field which would decide the fate of the world, with half a column devoted to his exploit in the Moniteur afterwards.

Aubard was the only man of the Fusiliers left mounted when the square broke. A rush of the Spanish lancers carried him away. He fought his way clear and rode to join the nearest rallying-group, but it surrendered before he reached it. He rode to join another, and was chased by a dozen yelling lancers. His splendid thoroughbred soon outdistanced their Lilliputian mounts, but he found himself a long way from the nearest French infantry by the time he had shaken off his pursuers. Then some irregular infantry began firing long shots at him, and he had to make a wide detour round them. Then more of the lancers crossed his path and headed him off. He saw the silver eagle which towered above one group of the Guard fall a second time, and it did not rise again.

He sat his horse disconsolate, the sword he was so proud of dangling idly in his hand, as he saw the last flurry of the battle under the scorching sun across the grey-green plain. Presumably he still could, had he chosen, have ridden into the Spanish ranks and hacked away with his sword until someone killed him, but it was not easy to decide to do it. No one could blame Aubard – he did not even blame himself – for wheeling his horse round and riding away from the scene of the defeat.

He was only twenty, and he wept as he rode away. The tears rolled down his cheeks. All that he had once been so proud of now seemed to be a mockery. His nodding bearskin and its scarlet plume, his blue uniform with its silver lace, his little scrubby moustache, so carefully tended – for no one might disfigure the ranks of the Guard with a bare upper lip – were all hateful to him now. It was not until an hour later, when his life was in danger again, that he forgot his unhappiness.

Aubard found a place where he could get his horse across the ravine. He rode hard for Salas; he nearly rode straight into a party of foragers from the besieging force, and was chased away along the Salas River. Forcing himself to be calm, he reined in his horse when he was once more safe and looked back at the distant fortress. The dust along the high road indicated the spot where the covering force – the force which had destroyed the Fusiliers – was marching back to join in the siege again. Besides them, there seemed to be several thousand men still round the fortress.

But to reach Salas was his only hope. Alone, and wearing his conspicuous uniform, he could not dream of riding back across Leon, or of riding forward over forty miles of unknown country to Valladolid. His one chance was that there was no strong force of the enemy on the other side of the Salas River opposite the fort.

Aubard reached Salas in safety in the end. He had to ride a long way up one bank of the river before he found a place to cross, and then he had to ride a long way back down the other side. Then at nightfall he had to turn his horse loose and scramble down the ravine to the rushing water in its rocky bed, and in the darkness he had to make his way, stumbling and slipping in his heavy boots along the stream to where the fortress towered above the bank. Then he climbed the bank with fearful difficulty – expecting every second to be observed and shot from the other side – and then, cowering at the foot of the wall, he had to call quietly until he attracted a sentry's attention, taking his chance lest the sentry should be one of the kind that fires first and challenges afterwards. He was nearly weeping again, with hunger and fatigue and cold, before they opened a postern to him and led him in to where General Meyronnet was waiting for news.

For Aubard had achieved something at least that day. He had brought the first authentic news out of Leon, the first real information which for three weeks or more had been able to trickle through the cordon of irregulars which the rebellion had called into being.

CHAPTER XXI

GENERAL COUNT DARPHIN woke with difficulty and realized that someone was pounding on his bedroom door.

"Who the devil's that?' he shouted, inhospitably.

'It's me, Guillermin,' said someone on the other side of the door.

'Oh, to hell with you,' said Count Darphin to himself, closing his eyes and promptly forgetting that Colonel Guillermin was anywhere near.

'Can't I come in? It's important,' persisted the pestilent Guillermin.

'Er – what?' asked Darphin, waking up again with a jerk.

'I want to come in,' said Guillermin.

'Confound these enthusiasts,' said Darphin to himself. He heaved himself out of bed, scuttled in his shirt across the floor and unlocked the door, and scuttled promptly back again and dived back into the warm comfort of the bed. It was still some time before dawn; only the faintest light was creeping in through the windows, and it was most savagely cold.

Colonel Guillermin came in slowly; although it was at such a ridiculous hour of the day he was dressed in the full uniform of the Imperial staff – the blue breeches with the gold stripe, the blue tunic covered with gold lace, the cloak trimmed with grey astrakhan; under his arm was the smart grey busby with its panache, and trailing at his side was the heavy oriental sabre which fashion had just decreed should be worn by staff officers.

'Take a chair,' said Darphin, shutting his eyes again. 'Make yourself quite comfortable, and then tell me what it is all about. More wails from the Army of Portugal again?'

'There are some complaints from the Prince of Essling,' agreed Colonel Guillermin, 'and something must be done about them. But I have something much more important to tell you.'

'Well, what is it?' said General Darphin, quite resigned.

But no words came to his listening ears for quite a time, and in the end Darphin opened his eyes again and craned his neck to peer over the sheets at him. Colonel Guillermin was gazing fixedly at the tumbled mass of black hair that lay on the pillow beside Count Darphin.

'Oh, never mind about Chuchita here,' said Darphin testily. 'She knows nothing of affairs, do you, my poupée?'

From under the bedclothes came the sound of the slap with which the general gave emphasis to his question and at the same time demonstrated his affection.

'No,' said Maria de Jesus – Chuchita for short – very sleepily, and the bedclothes heaved as she snuggled herself into a comfortable position with her head on the general's shoulder.

'So hurry up with this news of yours,' said the General.

'The news is from Leon,' said Guillermin; something in the quality of his voice would have told the general that the matter was of burning importance, pregnant with disaster, except that the general was still too sleepy to be receptive of minor details.

'News from Leon at last?' he said. 'What is it?'

'Leon is taken. Paris is dead – poisoned – and all the garrison with him. La Merced is taken. So are Mansilla and Saldaña. And the Fourth Fusiliers of the Guard were cut off in the plain and every man except one killed or taken. And there are ten thousand Spaniards besieging Salas at this moment.'

By the time the recital was finished Guillermin could have no cause for complaint regarding Darphin's lack of interest in what he was saying. Darphin was sitting bolt upright, having gradually pulled himself up to that position while Guillermin was adding horror to horror. And simultaneously with the rising of his body his jaw had fallen until his mouth was wide open. The natural disorder of his hair, of his heavy moustaches and whiskers, added to the ludicrous consternation of his expression.

'How do you know this is true?' demanded Darphin; but he showed his appreciation of the importance of the matter by flinging off the bedclothes – without a thought for the revelation of Chuchita's naked charms that ensued – and stepping out of bed.

'Meyronnet has sent the news from Salas. One of the Fusiliers got there after the regiment was destroyed – Salas is still open on the side of the river.'

Darphin pulled on his breeches.

'Have you told the marshal yet?' he asked.

'No,' said Guillermin with a trace of bitterness in his tone. One of the cast iron rules that General Darphin, as Chief of Staff to Marshal Bessières, had instituted, was that no one should dream of reporting direct to His Highness; it was significant that Darphin should have forgotten his own orders.

'I shall tell him at once,' said Darphin. 'Send to Dumoustier to tell him not to march this morning as last night's orders told him to. Send to Kellermann at Palencia to say he must be here with all his dragoons before nightfall tonight. Call Serras back too. The marshal will confirm in writing, but those messages must go in five minutes. Hurry!'

General Count Darphin had been a staff officer during nineteen years of continuous warfare. In the old revolutionary days the guillotine, and after that the Emperor's own drastic methods, had winnowed out the incompetents. Darphin knew his trade from beginning to end. The news that five thousand Frenchmen had been lost, that the communications were broken on which a quarter of a million French soldiers depended, left him unshaken. He might be growing old, careless, lazy, but there was nothing wrong with his nerve. Now that news had come through at last which cleared up the mystery as to what had been happening in Leon he took no longer than the time necessary to button his tunic to issue the orders which would set matters right. Yet he had to brace himself before going into the marshal's room with the news. His Highness

Marshal Bessières, Duke of Istria, Commander-in-Chief of the Army of the North of Spain, Colonel-General of Cuirassiers, Grand Eagle of the Legion of Honour, was not at all a sympathetic person in the matter of receiving bad news before breakfast. And Darphin positively shuddered at the thought of the letters, wild with wrath, which would come pouring in from Paris when communications should be reopened and the news should reach there of the destruction of one of the beloved regiments of the Guard.

While buckling his stock Darphin reached a new decision. He turned to where Chuchita lay motionless on the bed; he strongly suspected that she was motionless, enduring the cold of the morning on her naked body, because any attempt to pull the clothes up over herself would have reminded Darphin of her existence. Darphin was not nearly as much of a fool regarding Chuchita as Guillermin thought he was.

'I am sorry, Chuchita,' said Darphin slowly, 'but I don't want the news of this concentration to reach the Spaniards. It pains me to have to tell a lady that I do not trust her, but that is what my duty compels me to do. You will oblige me, my dear, by not going out of this room before this evening. In fact, I am going to post a sentry at the door in order to make certain of it. I regret very much causing you this inconvenience, but I am quite sure you appreciate the importance of the matter. Now calm yourself, my dear, and I will send some breakfast up to you.'

Perhaps it was Darphin's military training which had taught him when to make a judicious retreat; however it was, he decided in the face of the expostulations with which Chuchita proceeded to overwhelm him to finish dressing himself outside the room. He caught up his sword and his boots and scuttled through the door, and turned the key upon the bad temper which Chuchita was beginning to display. Rather than face it, he would prefer to endure the smiles of passers-by in the corridor while he pulled on his boots and buckled on his sword to the accompaniment of the drumming of fists upon the locked door.

And he held to his previous determination too, of posting a sentry at the door with orders to allow no one in or out. It was quite a shame that his motive should be misconstrued, that the sergeant of the guard should grin noticeably when he received the order. Fortunately General Darphin had forgotten any Latin he ever knew, and quite missed the point of the *sotto voce* remark of one of the aides-de-camp: *'Quis custodiet ipsos custodes?'*

To make quite certain that no hint of the blow that was intended should reach the Spaniards in the field he next sent orders to the guards at the gates. Until further orders no Spaniard was to be allowed outside the walls. Any citizen of Valladolid who wished to take the air must breathe the insanitary odours of his own alleys; any country man who wished to enter to sell his produce could only do so by resigning himself to an indefinite stay in the town.

With that settled, he went off to the barracks where Dumoustier's division, on receipt of the orders conveyed by Colonel Guillermin, had been dismissed from parade. Dumoustier's division was the finest of all the French Army of Spain, eleven battalions of the Young Guard, Voltigeurs, Tirailleurs, and Fusiliers. Dumoustier himself was sitting down to a second breakfast when Darphin entered – until ten minutes ago he and his men had been under orders to march south to join Masséna's army opposing Wellington.

'You will march north, not south, general,' said Darphin to Dumoustier. 'And you will not be starting until tomorrow night, after Serras and Kellermann have come in.'

'And why this change of plan?' asked Dumoustier.

'Leon has broken out, and wants taming all over again. You are just the man for the job, aren't you, general?'

'I have a reputation for taming provinces,' said Dumoustier.

He nodded his head slightly as if he were remembering past achievements; his eyes narrowed, and his lips revealed cruel white teeth under his black moustache. If Darphin had had any doubts as to the suitability of Dumoustier and his guard division for teaching Leon a lesson it would never forget they would have been instantly dispelled by the sight of the expression on Dumoustier's face. And when the Guard should hear of the annihilation of the Fourth Fusiliers . . . ! If there is any truth in the assertion that the contemplation of the sufferings of others help us to bear more easily our own suffering, General Darphin must have found much relief in thinking about what was going to happen to Leon while he bent his steps back to that dreaded interview with his commander-in-chief.

The latter was already worried enough by the news that Wellington was loose in the south; to hear that the devil was unchained in the north would rouse him to paroxysms of rage. For the splendid army which Masséna had led into Portugal the year before had now come reeling back again, starving, naked, with a third of its men and two-thirds of its horses dead of exposure and starvation before the Lines of Torres Vedras. Wellington, whom everyone had thought to be out of the game for good, was back again on the frontier of Spain. He was starving Almeida into surrender; he was threatening Ciudad Rodrigo with the same fate, and without prompt help from Bessières Masséna could do nothing to stop him.

So that letters had come pouring in to the Duke of Istria from the Prince of Essling, demanding clothing, food, guns, horses, and, above all, men, so that the insolent islanders could be thrust back into the mountains again. Phrases from the letters ran through Darphin's mind – 'You feed me only with promises'; 'You have used all sorts of pretexts to evade my requests'; 'Your letters are inconceivable'; 'All the troops in Spain are of the same family'; 'You are responsible for the defence of Almeida'; and so on interminably. And now at this very moment, when Dumoustier and Serras and Kellermann were all ready to march to Masséna's aid, and Masséna had been told to expect them, there came this news from the north.

There could be no hesitation about what to do. Every available man must be turned back to clear the communications. Not a man could be spared to help Masséna. What he would write when the news was broken to him Darphin could vizualize with extreme clarity. Not so definite but even more dreaded was the thought of what he should write to Paris regarding the shortcomings of Bessières and – for the greater includes the less – his chief of staff. The thought of it made Darphin's blood run cold; and he knew, even as he walked jauntily across the palace courtyard, that his chief would be equally apprehensive and consequently irritable.

To Darphin's credit it should be added that his fears were not entirely selfish. There were vague apprehensions regarding the future of France which worried him just as much however unacknowledged they might be. He could not conceive of an end to the glorious Empire; that the French dominion of Spain, even, should ever be seriously threatened was beyond the limits of his imagination. He would have laughed to scorn anyone who should suggest that no more than two years from now Wellington would sweep the French from the entire Peninsula in one brief campaign and come pouring triumphantly over the Pyrenees to deal the death wound to the Empire on the soil of France itself. All that would have seemed the merest rubbish to Darphin. But at the same time the thought of Wellington steadily extending his conquests, laying hold first of Almeida and then of Rodrigo, with the French powerless to keep him back, seemed strangely ominous and depressing to Darphin.

In that, of course, Darphin's military instinct was correct. The fall of Almeida was the beginning of that ebb tide which was to continue until the Allies should reach Paris. And Almeida fell because of the success of the revolt of the north. And it was the gun which was the cause of that success.

CHAPTER XXII

JORGE WAS pressing forward the siege of Salas with all the vigour that was in him and which his example could rouse in his men. He was having to learn the craft from first principles, but his was just the sort of temperament to which first principles make most appeal, and his immutable courage and endless cheerfulness set an example which his men were not slow to follow. Under the steady, deadly fire from the fortress the 'approaches' crept out from the 'first parallel'; two nights after the defeat of the Fusiliers of the Guard the 'second parallel' was begun and nearly completed, despite the fire of the besieged, and after daylight had come it was finished at the cost of much blood – a long, well planned trench with a solid parapet, which established the besiegers no more than two hundred yards from the walls. The howitzers within the fortress dropped shells into it with monotonous regularity, and the eighteen-pounders battered the parapets into ruin, but the Spaniards were not discouraged. They had been victorious too often lately for that. They pitched the corpses out over the back of the trench, and they rebuilt the parapet as fast as it was pounded down.

During the course of the day Jorge laboured over mathematical problems – as mathematics were a complete mystery to him he had to solve them by rule of thumb methods. Yet he was successful in his endeavours, for he was a man of hard common sense, and his experiences of the last few days had inspired him. When darkness fell fifty men crept over the parapet of the advanced trench and began to dig furiously, throwing up a thick parapet to enclose a small square battery on the baselines which Jorge, at the risk of his life, had marked out with stakes and tapes during the daylight. Ten men were levelling a section of the trench behind it. Ten more were levelling a section of the first parallel, so as to provide a passage for the big gun – a hundred men were dragging that up with drag-ropes.

Jorge managed somehow to be at all these places at the the same time. If when daylight came the gun had not reached the second parallel and the shelter of the battery, it would be pounded to pieces by the guns of the besieged as it stood exposed on the open ground. Similarly, if it reached the second parallel and the battery was not ready for it the same thing would happen. Everything must be completed to schedule. Jorge hurried back and forward, from the road to the second parallel, from the second parallel to the road, to keep everyone at work.

The besieged heard all the bustle and did their best to interfere. They rained shot and shell on the place where the sounds indicated that the battery was being dug. They changed their target and fired at the place where they could hear the noise of the dragging up of the big gun – one lucky round shot killed ten men in a line at one of the drag-ropes. They pushed out a sortie across no-man's-land, but of course Jorge had foreseen that possibility and had had a 'covering party' lying out there since nightfall; the brisk musketry fire that promptly spattered up caused the attackers to be withdrawn lest a trap had been laid for them.

Jorge had simply excelled himself. The big gun reached the first parallel just as the gap which was being made for it was completed; it was dragged across, and the trench instantly redug. He brought up a burdened carrying party with the huge baulks of timber – the rafter beams of a house – which were to act as flooring beneath the gun's wheels just as the redoubt was nearing completion, and no sooner had he got these laid when the gun itself was dragged in and put into position.

It was time enough, for it was nearly morning. Sweating with exertion and excitement Jorge made sure all was well. The men digging outside continued to cast up final spadefuls of earth on to the immense walls even when the growing light and the furious fire opened on the battery by the fortress made the work terribly dangerous. The work was finished as far as was necessary. The battery could boast of earthen walls immensely thick. It was not a thing of neat geometrical symmetry – unskilled enthusiasts working in pitch darkness could not produce that – but it would suffice. The gun rested on its timber platform two feet below the level of the ground. For five feet above ground level rose the walls, progressively thinner from below upwards. The embrasure through which pointed the muzzle of the gun was very narrow – the merest slit. That was all that was necessary, for the gun was only destined to fire at one single small portion of the wall, while the narrower the slit the less chance there was of lucky shots coming in through it.

Jorge had done well. An ordinary officer of engineers would most probably have consumed two nights in the construction of the battery, and a third in bringing up the gun. Jorge had telescoped three nights into one and had gained forty-eight hours. Already he was back on the road starting a fresh carrying party up the trenches – men carrying four roundshot apiece, slung over their shoulders, and barrels of powder. Hurrying back to the battery, Jorge issued instructions as to where his ammunition was to be stored; it must be in little parcels here and there along the trench near the battery but not too near; already a tornado of fire was opening upon the battery, and men, crouching in the bottom of the trench, were hurriedly filling sacks with earth with which to rebuild the walls as they crumbled beneath the cannon fire.

Then Jorge hurried off again and started men at work upon the new approaches. Two more trenches were to be run out from the second parallel, and then connected by a 'third parallel' close to the ditch. Here the storming party would assemble to attack the breach which the gun was to make; breach and parallel would have to be completed simultaneously. Jorge knew nothing of the refinements of siegecraft; he was not aware of the fact that in a properly conducted siege not only were the approaches carried up to the ditch, but the sides of the ditch and the obstacles in it should be levelled by mining, and the artillery fire of the besieged quite subdued before the breach should be stormed. These refinements were beyond Jorge's power, if not beyond his imagination. All he aimed at was to get a body of men near enough to a hole in the wall to have a chance of penetrating. The storm would be a bloody business – so would the approaching – but Jorge could not help that.

So all day long the approaches crept forward over the bare earth. Men were killed in them who had hardly had time to throw up ten spadefuls of earth. Men were buried under avalanches of earth and sandbags – the others only stopped to dig them out if to do so carried forward the work in hand. Dead bodies helped to give thickness to the parapets. The approaches at least served the purpose of multiplying the objectives of the besieged, so that the battery was not under such concentrated fire. Here the French were trying to drop shells into the work; but it was not so easy to drop a shell with indirect aiming into an area only ten feet square. French powder was not consistent enough, French shells were not cast truly enough, to make such accurate shooting likely – it was far otherwise with the magnificent English powder and shot which Jorge had at his disposal. Shells burst all round the battery; they burst on the very parapet, but the only one which fell inside failed to explode at once, and an imperturbable Galician vaquero who found the thing at his feet cut off the sizzling end of the fuse with a blow from his spade.

Meanwhile the gun had begun to fire back. Its bellowing roar, so well known to and so beloved by all the Spanish army, punctuated the fighting at regular intervals. Jorge was back with the gun again. It was he who squinted along the sights before each shot. And his inventiveness was developing hourly. Out of his own brain he had devised a system to limit the force of the recoil and minimize the labour of running up the gun each time. Behind the gun he had built up the timber platform in an inclined plane. At each shot the gun rolled backwards up it, hesitated, and then rolled forward again as gravity overcame the force of the recoil until it was almost in its correct firing position again. It almost doubled the speed of fire and halved the labour of handling the big brute.

Jorge was half mad with exultation and excitement. His face and hands were black with powder so that his eyes were unnaturally noticeable. He roared out bits of songs as he worked the gun. He slapped the big hot breech caressingly after each discharge. He did not seem to be fatigued, although he had fought a battle the day before and spent two consecutive nights in the most exhausting labour. He blazed away with the gun exultantly.

The effect of the battering upon the wall was small but all that could be hoped for. The solid stone splintered but little at each successive blow, but Jorge had thought out a scheme of battering which, significantly, exactly corresponded with the methods employed by the best schools of artillerymen. He was aiming at the foot of the wall, and he hoped, traversing the gun a little to right and to left, to undercut a section of it until the mass above it should come tumbling down, presenting a slope that should be easy of ascent; with luck the ruin should even fall into the ditch and lessen the difficulties of passing it. He had no idea how long this would take; all he knew was that he had the gun in position to contrive it sooner or later, and he was prepared to go on firing it until it happened.

He only left the gun at intervals to hurry along the trenches to where the murderous work of continuing the approaches was being carried on; he did this when he feared that the breach would be achieved before the third parallel could be completed. But sooner or later while he was at the approaches he became convinced that the third parallel would be completed before the wall should be breached, and so he hastened back to speed up the firing of the gun.

There were other interruptions. El Platero and Delgado and the others kept making their way up to the battery with complaints and requests. In the heat of all this fighting Jorge found himself beset with unending distractions. There were nearly ten thousand Spaniards grouped round Salas, and Jorge found himself in the semi-official position of commander-in-chief. He had to decide which sections of the army should man the trenches, and which portions of the trenches. He had to make arrangements for feeding them, sending out foraging parties on both sides of the road to bring in whatever provisions could be found. He had to see that provisions and water were carried up to the men in the trenches. He had to see that there was a sufficient force in support of the men in the trenches, lest the garrison should sally out and ruin everything. Jorge found himself not merely commander-in-chief, but his own chief of staff, his own artillery commander, his own chief engineer, his own chief commissary.

It was a matter of interest as to how long he would stand the strain. It was a significant fact that in the sweltering heat of the battery, with the gun bellowing its loudest and with shells dropping all round, Jorge was able to devise far more complicated arrangements and issue far more practicable orders than ever he would have been able to do if he had been peacefully herding sheep in the way he had spent most of his short life.

When night came, and he could no longer see the impact of the shot against the wall, so that he reluctantly decided to cease firing, he suddenly realized how exhausted and hungry he was. He braced himself to make his way again to the approaches, to warn the men there to make the most of the hours of darkness to push the works forward and to send patrols out to cover them, and then he picked his way back to the road where makeshift tents had been put up for Alvarez and the others, and where the men not in the trenches were preparing for another night's uncomfortable bivouac.

He asked for food, and they brought him some, bread and meat and wine, but he fell asleep as he ate. The wine in his cup cascaded over his breeches as his head fell forward on his knees, but he did not notice it. He rolled over on his side snoring with a noise like a badly blown trumpet, and Alvarez, who had come to love him, took off his own cloak to cover him. He lay there, and neither his own snores nor the constant passage to and fro of men and animals close by his head could wake him.

Yet at midnight something else woke him, so that he sat up with a jerk, with all his attention at stretch, like a wild animal. There was musketry fire from the trenches. It was no mere idle firing either, as might be expected if two patrols had met or a sentry had allowed his imagination to be too much for him. It was a well maintained blaze of musketry, and Jorge guessed what was its import. He leaped to his feet and ran for the trenches, stumbling in the darkness over obstacles innumerable. He fell headlong into the first parallel where men were peering over the parapet at the flashes of the firing, but he was on his feet again and shouting loudly before anyone could put a bayonet through him.

'Come with me, Princesa,' he yelled.

The men knew his voice. All along the trench in the darkness they followed the example of their neighbours and scrambled over the parapet and ran wildly forward, falling at length into the second parallel.

General Meyronnet in Salas had become really alarmed at the rapid advance of the siege works. At midnight he had sent out a strong sortie, which had overrun the patrols, had taken the approach trenches, where men were now busy shovelling down the parapets as fast as they could, and which had pushed a determined attack home upon the breaching battery intent upon capturing and disabling the one big gun which the besiegers possessed. Jorge and the Princesa Regiment arrived just as the attackers reached the second parallel. In the battery itself a grim fight was fought out in pitch darkness, where no one could tell friend from foe but struck and spared not. Jorge had been weaponless when he reached the battery, but somehow a spade had come to his hand and with this he fought murderously, sobbing with excitement, until he suddenly realized that the clamour had abruptly ceased with the flight or death of every Frenchman who had broken in.

In the darkness he felt his way to the gun, and ran his fingers anxiously over it. It was uninjured; he found the touch-hole and made sure no one had driven a spike into it; he ran his fingers along the chase to the muzzle; there was no crack or sign of injury. The trunnions were intact.

Satisfied in this, he only wanted to sleep again. He cared nothing for the fact that in the approach trenches there could still be heard shouts and shots as the last of the raiders were driven out by the Spaniards swarming up from the rear. He seated himself on the ground with his back to the trail of the gun and his shoulder against the wheel. He raised his head long enough to send an order to Elizalde regarding the manning of the trenches, and then he let it fall forward on to his breast again, and the sound of his snores filled the battery. Daylight revealed the extent of the damage. Great sections of the approach trenches had been tumbled down, so that it was impossible for men to reach the head of the sap under the fire of the besieged. There was a good many corpses littered between the trenches and the fort, and el Platero and several of his band were missing – the patrol he had been leading had been overwhelmed in the first rush, and el Platero was now somewhere in a dungeon of the fortress. If the place should be forced to surrender his life would be a valuable counter in the negotiations; if the besiegers should be driven off everyone knew what would happen to el Platero.

Jorge did not allow himself to be cast down; the sortie could have done far more damage than it did. He started the gun again at its work of battering, and went off to the approach trenches where he set the example of beginning the dangerous work of rebuilding the broken sections. The besieged had gained half a day for themselves by their sortie – it took that long before the sap heads could be reached again and the trenches pushed forward on their long-drawn zig-zag course towards the fort.

At midday something definite at last followed the discharge of the gun. There came a little avalanche of stone down from the face of the wall, the first indication that the gun was making an impression on the wall, twelve feet high and ten feet thick. Jorge rushed along to the sap head and stared at the wall. There was a little seam running up it now, like the trace of a water-course on the face of a cliff. At this distance of a hundred and fifty yards it was hard to be sure of details, but at any rate it was not now a smooth vertical ascent. There were at least projections and irregularities. A single man, active and unencumbered, might possibly climb it. That did not mean that an assault was possible in the face of a garrison a thousand strong, but it was at least a promise that a breach could be made sooner or later. And under the steady battering which went on during the rest of the day there were two or three further little avalanches. The wall was positively crumbling.

Jorge went back to the sap head to gaze at the wall again. It was dangerous work to show one's face there, for the garrison had lined the wall with musketeers, and at a hundred and fifty yards there was always a faint chance of a lucky shot – to say nothing of the fact that the besieged were always ready to pour in a torrent of grape if a fair enough target were offered.

Jorge came to the conclusion that another day's battering would pound ten feet of the wall into a practicable breach. He decided that that very night he must connect the advanced trenches with another parallel, a hundred yards or less from the ditch. And on the next night they would assault from there, with some chance of success. He left the men digging away at the sap head and proceeded back to the point on the road which a regular officer might have called 'headquarters', but which was actually only a convenient sort of rendezvous for everyone who had nothing special to do. His mind was busy with details; mentally he was allotting the various parts to be played that night by the different sections of the besiegers. Alvarez would have to take his men forward towards the wall as a covering party – irregulars were the best for that sort of night work. Princesa would, as usual, have to provide the four hundred men necessary for the digging; Elizalde would have to allot the task to whichever battalion he thought fit. In the second parallel and the first parallel there would be – Jorge was interrupted in his thoughts by a hand laid upon his arm. He turned and found one of the boys who composed the gun crew; he was out of breath with running after him and his lips trembled.

'The gun, señor!' he said. 'The gun!'

'What about the gun?' demanded Jorge, with sudden fear at his heart.

The boy stammered and gesticulated, but he could not utter a word more of sense. With a curse Jorge turned away from him and began running heavily back to the battery, and what he found there was worse than he had anticipated. There were dead men there, but Jorge cared nothing for dead men. The gun, his beautiful big gun, was out of action. The carriage still stood, somehow, although half of one tall wheel was shattered. But the gun itself was tilted up at a grotesque elevation, and at the same time was twisted over on its side. One trunnion had been smashed clean off – the raw irregular surface of the broken metal was visible. The elevating gear and the training gear were now only represented by splinters of wood and distorted bars of metal. On the chase a wide area of the ornamental relief work had been ploughed off.

Jorge stood glaring at the ruin. He could not see how it happened. The explanation was brought home to him a second later. There was a howl like that of a thousand lost souls, and a wind that flung him back against the battery wall. A big cannon ball had entered by the embrasure as its predecessor must have done, but this one had gone clean across the battery from front to back without hitting anything. Jorge peered through the embrasure. On the top of the fortress wall, silhouetted against the evening sky, he saw a black hump close above the point where the breach was being made; it had not been there when he had looked half an hour before from the sap head. It was a big gun, foreshortened, pointing straight at him.

For all the anguish which afflicted him Jorge could picture what the French had been doing – he knew much about the handling of heavy artillery nowadays. Finding that no gun of theirs would bear so as to fire into the embrasure they must have set to work instantly building a ramp up the inside of the wall, with a platform at the upper end just below the top of the wall, and they had dragged one of their eighteen-pounders up the ramp to the platform. As soon as it reached there they had swung it round and begun firing into the battery. Now that Jorge looked closer he could see men's heads bobbing about round the gun as they reloaded it. Instinct caused him to pull down his head and crouch below the embrasure as the next shot was fired. There was a crash behind him, a ringing noise as though a great bell had been struck with a sledge hammer; a sizzling fragment of metal sang over his shoulder and buried itself in the battery wall close by his face. Jorge turned to see that the wreck of the gun was completed. The ball had hit the under side of the chase, making a great dent, and flinging down the gun from the wrecked carriage. Its breech had fallen on the ground and its muzzle perched up on the axle; the lettering round it in its old-fashioned Latin characters still said, 'And our mouths shall show forth Thy praise'.

CHAPTER XXIII

AT NIGHTFALL there was a good deal of activity among the besiegers of Salas. The gun would never fire again and the rumour of that had gone round the ranks, but they were in too high spirits still to be discouraged at the thought of that. Everyone could appreciate the desirability of capturing a fortress which completely commanded the whole line of communications of the enemy, and flesh and blood were to finish off the work the gun had begun. Salas was to be stormed that night. The men were to attack in the darkness, over a deep ditch, up a wall like a cliff. The wall was seamed by one tiny crack; besides that they had a dozen ladders taken from the farms nearby. Nevertheless the men had not the least doubt that they were going to succeed; their commanders naturally did not communicate their doubts on the subject to them.

In gloomy conference they had settled the details – Alvarez was to assail the breach, and Elizalde was to attack at one side and the rest of the Princesa Regiment at the other, while Jorge led the irregulars round in an attack upon the river face of the fortress. In the darkness they moved the columns of men up to the second parallel – that was difficult enough in itself – and some time after midnight they streamed out to the attack.

There is no need to dwell upon the details of that repulse. The French in Salas had given proof enough already of their activity and vigilance and courage. Only against a craven enemy, demoralized and unready, could the assault have succeeded. The summit of the wall blazed with the fire of the besieged as the Spaniards approached. Grape and canister from the guns mounted to sweep the foot of the walls tore the Spaniards to pieces. Tar barrels and bundles of oily rags, all aflame, were flung down from the walls and served to give sufficient illumination to the musketeers upon the wall. Live shells with short fuses, dropped down by hand, blew apart the little groups of Spaniards who reached the foot of the wall. Fanatical courage brought them up to the attack over and over again; until towards morning the courage suddenly evaporated, as it will do with undisciplined troops, and they broke and flew away from the walls in blind terror, leaving even the trenches deserted, and only the dead and wounded piled upon the glacis as proof of what they had dared before this panic overtook them.

In the grey morning Jorge came back from the wall where he had raged berserk but uselessly, and found

Alvarez and the others at the roadside. He halted his men and bade them rest – the survivors of el Bilbanito's band, and O'Neill's band, and el Platero's band were very, very few now – while he went up to the conference. Alvarez' right arm was in a sling, and his clothes were in rags. Elizalde was in as bad a condition. Only Urquiola was as spruce and smart as ever, because his cavalry had taken no part in the assault.

'Delgado is dead,' said Elizalde.

'Yes,' said Jorge.

'So is Volpe.'

'So are half my men,' said Alvarez, 'but I write no poems about it.'

Jorge looked back at the fortress, at the low grey wall just visible over the rolling plain. Even at that distance he could see the speck which floated above it – the tricolour on its invisible staff.

Alvarez broke in upon the reverie into which Jorge was imperceptibly drifting.

'Holy Mary,' said Alvarez. 'Here comes a bird of ill omen.'

They looked southward down the road as he pointed; a big man on a little white mule, his skirted legs trailing on each side so far down that his feet almost brushed the road, was riding up towards them. They saw the brownish grey habit, and the massive black beard. It was Brother Bernard.

No one wanted to listen to Brother Bernard at that moment. They moved restlessly under his reproaches when he heard the news, like lions beneath the lion-tamer's whip. They sulked and they snarled. They had done all that men – men without a gun – could do, and they resented bitterly his recriminations. They thought of the dead men along the foot of the wall, and Jorge thought of the gun, broken and grotesque, deserted in its battery.

'And the French will be here tomorrow from Valladolid,' said Brother Bernard.

Alvarez looked up with a start.

'*Who* will be here?' he demanded.

Brother Bernard had not been idle, it appeared, while they had been pouring out their blood round the walls of Salas. He had seen the army of relief start out from Valladolid. He had watched them all one day; he knew just how the army was composed, and he had ridden hard all night to bring the news. Every unit, every general in the French army, was known to Brother Bernard. The names he let fall were as well known to his listeners. They had all heard of Kellermann and his dragoons – Urquiola had been hunted by them times without number across the plains of Castile which Kellermann ruled. And Dumoustier and the Guard division; Dumoustier was the name Spanish women used to frighten their children. Serras, too; small imagination was required to picture Dumoustier and Serras turned loose to subjugate Leon. Twelve thousand infantry, three thousand cavalry and a dozen guns; there would be fire and rape and slaughter from here to the Cantabrian mountains.

And the connecting link which might have held the army together in face of this danger was broken. The gun was a gun no longer, and the courage and good spirits which the gun had brought into existence had vanished last night under the walls of Salas. Alvarez was thinking about the charges Kellermann's dragoons could deliver here on these naked plains.

'I shall take my men back to Navarre while the road is still clear,' he said. 'I know the by-ways past Burgos. Mina only gave me leave to help el Bilbanito for three months, and the three months are ended.'

The others looked at him, but he was quite brazen about his motives.

'I risked my men in a forlorn hope last night,' he said, 'but it would be worse than a forlorn hope to try and defend Leon against Kellermann and Dumoustier. And only the hope of seeing Navarre again speedily will keep my men together. I shall march in an hour's time.'

Urquiola looked automatically at his big silver watch.

'If Kellermann has left Castile,' he said, 'my place is there. Our business is to be where the French are not. In a week's time I shall be raiding up to the gates of Madrid.'

'And what about Leon?' asked Brother Bernard.

Urquiola hesitated before he enunciated the heartless truth.

'Leon must look after itself,' he said.

The madness which underlay Brother Bernard's enthusiasm for the cause broke its bonds. He raised his clenched hands above his head.

'Woe unto you,' he said, 'May God —'

Urquiola and Alvarez bore his curses as philosophically as a resigned husband bears the scoldings of his wife, and listened as heedlessly. The bonds of union had snapped with the disabling of the gun; and moreover there were sound military arguments in favour of a prompt dispersal in face of the overwhelming force of the enemy.

And while Brother Bernard was calling down upon Urquiola and Alvarez the enmity of God, Jorge slipped unobtrusively away. It was not his duty, nor that of any irregular, to stand a siege by a French army. Jorge was determined not to be shut up in Leon or Saldaña or La Merced to await inevitable death or captivity. He thought of his native Cantabrian mountains. He had a horse still, which was far more than he had had when he descended from them. The relics of the guerillero bands would follow him if he promised to lead them back home. The Princesa Regiment – what was left of it – and the Leonese levies could obey Brother Bernard if they wished. As for him, he was off home. He had had his fill of commanding an army.

Over by the deserted trenches, foul with dead bodies, a

patrol from Salas climbed cautiously over into the battery. They examined curiously the huge bronze gun which lay wrecked upon the splintered flooring. A scholar among them looked at the half defaced heraldic traceries upon it, but he did not know which ducal house it was which bore those arms. He was able to puzzle out the Latin of the legend round the muzzle, and he translated it for his comrades, who were much amused. But still, the gun had played its part in history.

Nevile Shute
The Far Country £2.95

Australia – the land of opportunity, and a place to build a new life in a new world

For Carl Zlinter, the Czech doctor, the end of the war and his move to Australia signals a period of unexpexcted hope. It is a time for exploration – together with Jennifer Morton, young, lovely and far from her English home.

But Carl is not all that he seems, and even Jennifer is not privy to his dark secret. A secret that, when exposed, theatens to shatter all his dreams and expectations.

'Full of drama . . . a most satisfying and human book' PUNCH

'Fine people and a brave book' NEW YORK TIMES

The Rainbow and the Rose £2.50

'There is great strength and great tenderness in Nevil Shute's tale. It concerns real people in a real world and it is steeped in a sense of their poetry and their romance' EVENING NEWS

Requiem for a Wren £2.50

The silent tensions of everyday life in England before D-Day. A story of friendship and enduring love, which begins when a young Wren meets two Australian servicemen as the invasion fleet masses. The events of these crowded days are told with a compassionate brilliance.

'His best since *A Town Like Alice*' OBSERVER

John le Carré
The Honourable Schoolboy £3.50

'The ultimate espionage novel. London, Hong Kong, Vientiane are the settings and George Smiley and company are back . . . It is hard to see how even le Carré could surpass himself after this' PUBLISHERS WEEKLY

'One of the most effective thrillers we have had for years. His command of detail is staggering, his straightforward, unaffected prose is superb. In short, wonderful value' SUNDAY TIMES

'Compassionate, distinguished, terrifying' COSMOPOLITAN

The Little Drummer Girl £3.50

'The scene is England, West Germany, Greece, Israel and the Palestinian camps. The story has to do with an appealing, if rather aimless, young English actress who is recruited by an Israeli intelligence team to infiltrate a Palestinian terrorist group and lead them to its leader. How this recruitment is accomplished and how her infiltration is achieved are dazzling, hypnotically gripping' NEW YORKER

Le Carré's most ambitious piece of writing in twenty years of considerable achievement' OBSERVER

The Spy Who Came In From The Cold £2.95

A topical and terrible story of an Egnlish agent . . . the monstrous realities behind the news paragraphs which record the shifts and tensions of the Cold War . . .

'Superbly constructed, with an atmosphere of chilly hell' J. B. PRIESTLEY

Tinker Tailor Soldier Spy £3.50

'. . . plenty of flashback travel . . . interdepartmental skulduggery . . . rapid action at intervals and a red peppering of violence' OBSERVER

'There is a depth of characterization in Tinker Tailor Soldier Spy that you will find in no other espionage novels, and actually in few novels of any sort today' WASHINGTON POST

John Steinbeck
East of Eden £3.95

The famous saga of the Trasks and the Hamiltons who grew up in the Salinas Valley between two major wars. From its masterly portrayal of Cathy – adultress and murderess – to its graphic presentation of conflict between brother and brother; from its glittering vignettes of Californian small-town life to its panoramic fresco of a growing nation, *East of Eden* is an unforgettable reading experience.

The Grapes of Wrath £2.95

The story of the great migration of thousands of homeless families from the dust-bowl of Oklahoma to California. It traces the fortunes of the Joad family who, lured by the promise of unlimited work, head for the 'Golden West', the land of plenty – only to find their hopes shattered as they encounter bitter poverrty and oppression . . .

'This is a terrible and indignant book; yet it is not without passages of lyrical beauty, and the ultimate impression is that of the dignity of the human spirit under the stress of the most desperate conditions' GUARDIAN

Of Mice and Men £1.50

This is the story of Lennie, one of Steinbeck's most poignant characters. A simple-minded giant, Lennie must rely on George, his mentor and protector . . . But even his best friend cannot save Lennie from his worst enemy – his own strength . . .

'His just understanding of character, the candour and forcefulness of his dialogue and his mastery of climaxes are all his own and inimitable' TIMES LITERARY SUPPLEMENT

W. Somerset Maugham
The Razor's Edge £2.95

The story of three of Maugham's most brilliant characters – Isabel,
whose choice between passion and wealth has lifelong
repercussions . . . her uncle, Elliot Templeton, a classic American
snob . . . and Larry Darrell, Isabel's ex-fiancé who leaves his
stockbroking life in Chicago to seek spiritual peace in a Guru's *ashram*
in Southern India.

The Moon and Sixpence £2.50

Based on the life of Paul Gauguin, *The Moon and Sixpence* is the story
of Charles Strickland, a London stockbroker who suddenly abandons
his wife and family, to become a painter in Tahiti. Here is a portrayal of
the mentality of genius – and a brilliant affirmation of Maugham's
power as a novelist.

The Narrow Corner £2.50

This tale of the sea came from a passage in *The Moon and Sixpence*
which Maugham had written twelve years earlier. The villainous
Captain Nichols brings his passenger, Fred Blake, a fugitive from the
law, to the remote island of Kanda after a violent storm – and what
starts as a thrilling tale of sea adventure becomes a tragic tale of
love . . .

Of Human Bondage £3.95

In this, perhaps the most famous of Somerset Maugham's novels, we
follow the story of Philip Carey, an orphaned cripple, in his quest for
life and love. Turning from the bohemian life of a Parisian art student
and the demands of the tragic Fanny, he studies medicine in London,
where Mildred, superficial but irresistible, nearly brings about his ruin.

All these books are available at your local bookshop or newsagent, or can be ordered direct from the publisher. Indicate the number of copies required and fill in the form below.

Send to: **CS Department, Pan Books Ltd., P.O. Box 40, Basingstoke, Hants. RG21 2YT.**

or phone: 0256 469551 (Ansaphone), quoting title, author and Credit Card number.

Please enclose a remittance* to the value of the cover price plus: 60p for the first book plus 30p per copy for each additional book ordered to a maximum charge of £2.40 to cover postage and packing.

*Payment may be made in sterling by UK personal cheque, postal order, sterling draft or international money order, made payable to Pan Books Ltd.

Alternatively by Barclaycard/Access:

Card No. | | | | | | | | | | | | | | | | |

Signature:

Applicable only in the UK and Republic of Ireland.

While every effort is made to keep prices low, it is sometimes necessary to increase prices at short notice. Pan Books reserve the right to show on covers and charge new retail prices which may differ from those advertised in the text or elsewhere.

NAME AND ADDRESS IN BLOCK LETTERS PLEASE:

....

Name ⎯⎯⎯⎯⎯⎯⎯⎯⎯⎯⎯⎯⎯⎯⎯⎯⎯⎯⎯⎯⎯⎯⎯⎯⎯⎯

Address ⎯⎯⎯⎯⎯⎯⎯⎯⎯⎯⎯⎯⎯⎯⎯⎯⎯⎯⎯⎯⎯⎯⎯

⎯⎯⎯⎯⎯⎯⎯⎯⎯⎯⎯⎯⎯⎯⎯⎯⎯⎯⎯⎯⎯⎯⎯⎯⎯⎯⎯⎯

⎯⎯⎯⎯⎯⎯⎯⎯⎯⎯⎯⎯⎯⎯⎯⎯⎯⎯⎯⎯⎯⎯⎯⎯⎯⎯⎯⎯

3/87